Kansaska

a novel

Kansaska

a novel

Jeff Stanger

Indianapolis, Indiana

Acknowledgements:

Thanks to the team behind the book:

Lorrie Algate- Editing, cheerleading and having the good
sense to have relatives in Kansas and Nebraska.

Terry Sowka- Editing, fact checking, quality control, and
knowing state capitals.

Justin Bessler- Cover design, interior layout, logos, working
for food.

Brian Groce- All things web and technical. A geek's geek
to be sure.

Marjorie Kirkpatrick- Official Historian of Kansaska

The names of the baseball teams in this novel came about as the
result of a contest. The following winners should be noted both for
their creativity and their apparent abundance of free time.

PARALLEL LIONS by Amanda Groce

MOONLIGHT SONATAS by Delana Bradbury

GENEVA GNOMES by Linda Wright

MCPHERSON MARAUDERS by Julie.

BEAVER CITY FUR TRADERS by Mark Jenkins AND

BEAVER CITY BEAVERS by Gene Fitzpatrick

RED CLOUD ARROWHEADS by Marjorie Kirkpatrick

MINDEN APPLEPICKERS by Erin Benziger

FAIRBURY GRAVEDIGGERS by Justin Bessler

VESPER TURKEY VULTURES by Jarrod Harvey

Introduction

I became friends with my Uncle George during the summer of 1997. Of course, he was dead by then, so we didn't talk much. I met him when I was a kid, but I never really knew him until Roxy, my grandmother, read aloud his memoirs during the summer the town of Bloomington, Indiana, tried to buy the Dodgers. Over the course of two evenings in June, she shared his adventures while we sat on her screened-in porch.

As she read, kids from the neighborhood played Wiffle Ball® in the side yard. By the end of the second evening, the kids were crowded on the porch with us. I think Uncle George's story is a good one, although I'm not sure I believe it all, what with the aliens and the Canadians and the gypsies. But it's a good story nonetheless. It's too bad Roxy isn't around to read it to you.

Andy Bennett

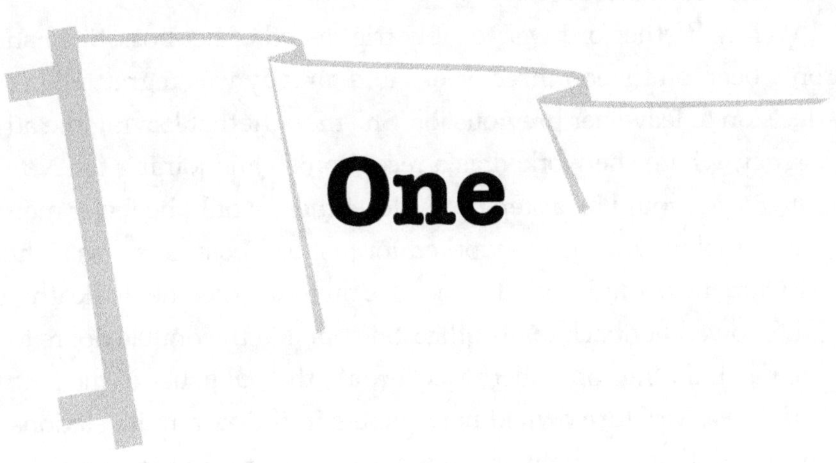

One

"George, Mr. McClure wants to see you right away."

"What kind of mood is he in?" I asked.

"His face is red, his tie is undone, and he's already drinking gin," answered McClure's personal assistant.

"That's not good."

"George, are you still going steady with Thelma?" she asked.

"Yes."

"That's why his face is red. Are you still working on the Joe DiMaggio story?"

"Yes."

"That's why his tie is undone. Are you still planning on marrying his daughter?"

"Yes."

"That's why he's drinking gin. Well, get in there before he

becomes even more cross."

Wendy Wetherford was terribly frightened of her boss. She had only been on the job three weeks and already was regretting her decision to leave her previous job. She thought that leaving the ad agency, where she worked as a receptionist, and joining the *New York Bugle*, would be a step up. At least there would be fewer men with grabby hands if she worked for just one boss. She was right. McClure never laid a hand on her. He merely scared her to death.

I followed her back to his office. She opened the double doors to the palatial office of Hubert McClure IV, the publisher of the *New York Bugle*. McClure owned newspapers in the east, radio stations in the west, and a chain of grain and feed stores in between. The McClure family built a fortune in farming supplies, dating back to the 1800's. His grandfather added to their wealth by buying newspapers and his father increased the family fortune by buying radio stations.

"Bennett!" he screamed. "Sit down."

"Yes sir, I—"

"Don't talk, just listen. Is it true that you gave my daughter, Thelma, an engagement ring?"

I stared back at him.

"Well, answer me."

"You said not to talk, just listen."

"Don't be a wise guy. Answer the question."

"Yes sir. I did give her a ring."

"And did I give you permission? Did you ask for my blessing? What kind of a man are you?"

What kind of a man was I? I hadn't really thought much about it before. A fellow just kind of "is" sometimes. He's not thinking about what he is, he just is. I left Indiana after high school and came to New York. I started working for the Bugle while going to NYU.

Once I graduated to the Yankees beat, I quit school. I usually stick with things, but I was only going to school to become a baseball writer anyway. So, what was the point of staying in college?

It didn't take a long time at the Bugle to notice Thelma. She made an impression on me the first day in May of 1947. I had stepped onto the elevator and heard running footsteps behind me. The elevator operator looked me in the eyes and said, "Duck."

I didn't duck. Thelma stepped onto the elevator, spun around to face the door, swung the seven bags she was carrying and plopped them on the floor. It was the purse that got me. The strap was around her neck because of the other bags. When she spun around, the purse circled her body until it collided with my head.

From the floor, I looked up at the elevator operator. He smiled and said, "I told you to duck."

I decided that day that he and I would be mortal enemies. It was as if he had watched this hurricane of a woman send men to the floor with aching heads before. Yet, he gave his cryptic one-word warning that he knew wouldn't be heeded. I concluded this moment of wicked joy became the highlight of a day otherwise spent riding up and down in a little closet. His only fringe benefit was seeing the spectacle of Thelma McClure nearly decapitate the unsuspecting men of the *New York Bugle*.

Of course, when Thelma realized there was a man writhing in pain below her feet, she quickly apologized and offered to make up for the offense. The only suitable restitution I could suggest, upon actually seeing her face, was for her to accept my invitation to dinner. The evening together proved to be most delightful and I soon found myself courting this magnificent creature. As far as I could tell, she was perfect in almost every way. I say almost because she did happen to be the clumsiest debutante to graduate finishing school.

Her only other flaw was her lack of foresight in her choice of a father. Why did she have to be the boss's daughter? And why didn't he like me?

Before I could ponder that question, I realized he was still waiting for my response. "I'm the kind of man who would make any girl's father proud. Please sir, give me a chance. Give me a chance to prove that I am the man for your daughter," I pleaded.

"All right then, Bennett, I'm sending you to the K.R.A.P. League."

"Figuratively or literally, sir?"

"Both. You're going to run the Portis Eskimos in the Kansaska Retail Agriculture Products League."

"The Portis Eskimos?"

"That's right, Portis, Kansas. I have two teams in the K.R.A.P. League." He stared out the window. I assume he was looking at Portis, or at least in the general direction of Portis. "You will, of course, be running the worst one. Portis has not had a winning season in 19 years. I never minded because the folks 'round there had nothing better to do, so they still came to the games."

He went on to explain that I would be responsible for managing the day-to-day operations of the team and also have to work at the feed store. Apparently, the previous business manager for the team had lost a lot of McClure's money. He knew I didn't have a business background. This was his way of guaranteeing that I would fail and do it on such a grand scale that Thelma would lose interest.

McClure had a giant framed map of the United States above a leather couch. I studied Kansas until he finished talking. "I can't seem to find Portis on your map, sir."

"That's because Portis isn't on most maps. Look on this one behind my desk."

Sure enough, marked by red and blue pushpins, Portis was on the special map. "The blue pins are where I have businesses and the red pins are towns with teams in the league."

As I studied the town names, I realized the shape of the league roughly formed a heart extending to the middle of Nebraska while the "v" shape at the bottom of the heart cut a wedge out of Kansas.

"Of course in Red Cloud, Nebraska, are the Arrowheads. They are my pride and joy. They have won six league titles including the past two years. The team is run by Rodney Sparks, nephew of Randolph Sparks. Do you know that name?"

"No, sir, I don't."

"Randolph Sparks is the tractor king of the Midwest. Why, half the farmers in the country ride his tractors and the other half are just saving up to buy one. You can't compete with that, George."

"I can't?"

"No. I don't mind telling you Rodney is the man for my daughter — even if she is too blind to see it. Someday, Rodney will take over my entire Agricultural Products Division. That is if he doesn't run for Congress. And mind you, he could. He has the money, friends, and ambition to do it. Rodney is Yale educated. What was that college you dropped out of?" He did not wait for me to answer. "He has power and class. You possess none of these things, young man. He is going to be a huge success. Already is, in fact. What are you going to be?"

Again, he did not allow me to answer. "Therefore, I am giving you a challenge: win the pennant and keep the team in the black, and you will have my blessing to marry my daughter. Fail and you lose her, not to mention the fact that the Eskimos will melt away. I cannot support two teams anymore. You put people in the seats or I'll fold that team."

"What if I refuse to go along with your plan and marry your daughter anyway?"

"Do you really think I would let that happen? Do you really think

I won't use all the power and money at my disposal to ruin you if you tried?"

"Why are you doing this to us, Mr. McClure? Don't you love your daughter?"

That question made him angry. "How I show my love to my daughter is none of your damn business. Besides, having her marry the successful heir to the Randolph Tractor business is a lot more loving than letting her marry a baseball beat writer on one of my newspapers.

"It's because of her, and her mother, that I'm doing this. Believe me, if I could, I would fire you right now. No, I need you to fail or she is never going to get you out of her system.

"Of course, I could offer you an alternative." He lowered his head and looked up over his glasses. "I could make it worth your while to call off the engagement and end your relationship with my daughter."

I did not answer. The sun went behind a cloud, making his office as dark as his heart. "Everyone knows that Russell is going to retire in May. You could jump ahead of all those reporters who have paid their dues. You could be the sports editor of the *New York Bugle*. It is the plum sports job in the greatest city in the world. All you have to do is foreswear my daughter. You will be famous and well compensated. Or, you can spend a summer in Kansas — away from your beloved Yankees during the year they celebrate the 25th anniversary of Yankee Stadium."

He knew how to push my buttons. This was shaping up to be a dream season for Yankee fans.

"Rumor has it they are going to retire Ruth's number this summer, too," he continued. "What is it going to be, boy? The prestige, the money, and the Yankees, or a summer in Kansas?"

"Aren't you forgetting about the most important part of this?

Your daughter?"

"Of course not. However, this is business. What do you say, Mr. Editor?"

The grin of the devil himself settled on the face of McClure. I held out my hand to shake his and he chuckled proudly. When he took my hand, I pulled him in close and hissed at the devil, "I'm going to Portis."

In a rage, he pushed by me and stomped towards the door. He flung it open and pointed to the hall.

"Get out of here, you fool. The season starts in three weeks, so you had better catch the next train out of here. However, if you choose to go on with this marriage, you will be terminated. In addition, if you pop up at any other newspaper in North America, I will buy it and fire you again. Now get out of my office — and finish that damn DiMaggio story!"

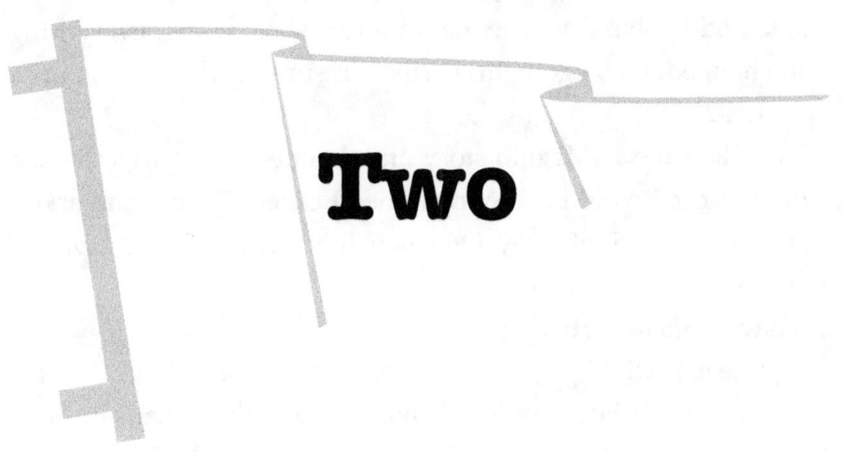

Two

I walked out of the office and waved at Wendy. "I'm glad you made it out alive, George," she said, consolingly.

"Wendy, have you ever heard of Portis?"

"Is that the disease where your skin turns yellow?"

"No, that's jaundice. Portis is in Kansas."

"Oh. Do people in Kansas have yellow skin?"

I thought about the question for a moment. "I'm going there very soon. I'll let you know," I answered.

I went back to my desk and thought about McClure's challenge. It was absurd that in 1948, two adults couldn't get married. Sure, there was nothing legally preventing us from getting married, but McClure's power superseded the law. And besides, as crazy as it seemed, I found myself yearning for a chance to prove myself.

When I had woken up that morning, I thought I knew who I was and where I was going. My destination: Sports Editor of the Daily Bugle and husband to Thelma. In a few short hours, everything had changed. Was I going to Portis to insure my destination or in spite of it?

I finished the DiMaggio story and wondered if it was the last Yankee piece I would ever write. Then I called Thelma and asked her to meet me right away. On a bench in Central Park I gave her the news.

"I have to go to Portis."

"Where is Portis?"

"I was hoping you would tell me. I know it's in Kansas. Your father owns a feed store there."

"Oh, I haven't traveled to any of his businesses in the Midwest since I was a little girl. He took me by train on one of his business trips. Why does he want you to go to Portis?"

"So we can be married."

Thelma's eyes widened. "He knows?"

"Yes."

Thelma knew what that meant. McClure had expressed his disapproval of our relationship on previous occasions. He once threatened to fire me over it, but an attempt to unionize the newspaper's workers distracted him.

As a family outsider, I always thought that Thelma and her father had a strange relationship. Her mother had died in a car accident when Thelma was only three years old. Her father never remarried, although there always was a Manhattan socialite on his arm when he was seen in public.

McClure was at a loss when it came to raising his daughter, so he hired a nanny and spoiled Thelma with his considerable wealth. While that combination would have doomed most women to a life of narcissism and excess, she was kept in check by the gentle wisdom of her nanny.

She called her nanny Grandma Esther. Esther was a Jewish immigrant who left Persia after the 1921 coup. She instilled in Thelma a sense of duty to the poor and others rejected by mainstream society that stayed with her into adulthood. Those packages Thelma was carrying the day we collided were for poor women who never would be allowed in an upscale New York department store.

Grandma Esther also fueled a passion for education that took Thelma to college. She became a photojournalist, winning an award for her photo series on the work of The Salvation Army in New York City.

Thelma stared back at me for a moment. "What does Portis have to do with our getting married?"

"Your father won't give us his blessing unless I go to Portis and run his baseball team."

"He has a baseball team?"

"Yes, he has two. The other is in Red Cloud, Nebraska."

Her eyes grew wide when I mentioned Red Cloud. Neither one of us had to say a thing. She knew who was in Red Cloud, even if she had not previously cared why.

"He's running the team in Red Cloud isn't he?"

"Yes."

"I suppose he told you how Rodney is so much better for me than you or any other man?"

"He sure did. Rodney has quite an impressive resume."

"And my father wants you and Rodney to compete for me using the baseball teams."

"Yes."

"No."

"Huh?"

"No, I refuse." She sat back on the bench, crossed her arms and shook her head. "I'm not going to do it. I'm not going to be the prize at the end of the season." She paused and shook her finger at me, "Not a chance, Mr.. We are getting married whether he likes it or not. And no baseball game—"

"Season."

"—season is going to interfere with it."

"We have no choice."

"You don't mean to sit there and tell me you are actually going to go through with this?"

"What choice do we have? He is the most powerful man in New York! Even the mayor is afraid of him. He'll fire me and make sure I never work for another paper in the city."

"Fine, we will leave New York. You could work at a paper in Philadelphia or how about Baltimore?"

"He would just buy that paper and fire me."

"Whoever gave you that idea?"

"Actually, he did. Those were his exact words."

She paused and considered the source. "He does hold a grudge, but what if you lose?"

"Lose?" The consequence had not crossed my mind.

"What if you lose? Then you and my father just hand me over to Rodney like a trophy?"

"I guess I'm just not thinking about the worst right now. I'm trying to stay positive."

She moved towards the edge of her seat. "Well, how good is this team?"

"They haven't had a winning season in nineteen years."

She fell back and said, "George, this is hopeless. Why go through with it?"

"Because, maybe just trying will impress him. Maybe I can win him over."

"You've won me over. Isn't that all that matters?"

"So, you would rather elope?"

"Yes."

"Darling, think of all the things you would have to give up."

"I'm not that close to my father anyway."

"I mean the other things."

"What other things?"

"You know — New York things."

"Such as?"

"Your friends, Broadway shows, the shopping, the restaurants…"

She grabbed my arm and looked me in the eyes. "You're going to need some help packing. How long did you say you would be gone?"

I was a bit taken aback by her response, but then I saw the laughter in her eyes.

"George, you know those things don't mean anything to me compared to you. But I can tell that you feel like this is something you have to do."

I smiled at her in relief. "I'm very glad you're being so gracious about this."

She winked at me. "Actually I know you well enough to know that no matter what I do to try to convince you to stay, you're stubborn enough to go any way. With or without my blessing. So it's just easier for both of us if I pretend it was my idea."

I hugged her tight. "You're a very smart woman. Now, did you say you would help me pack?"

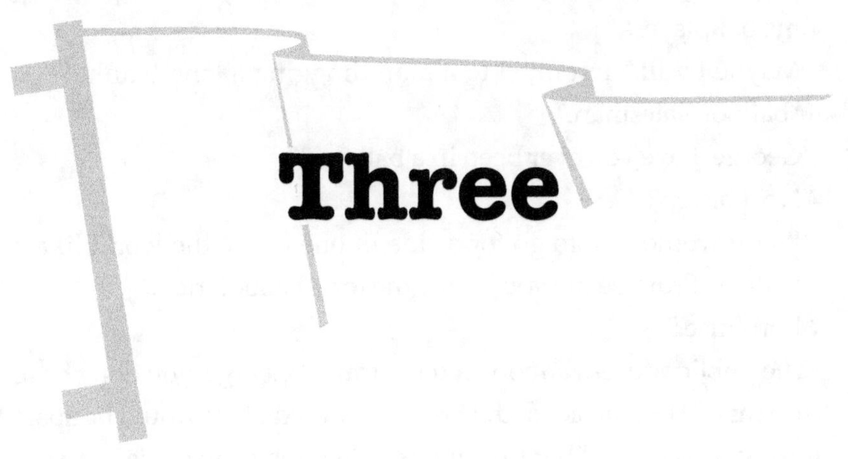

Three

T helma and I sat together on a bench in Grand Central Station. We both liked to watch people. All sorts of folks were coming and going at the train station. We tried to imagine where they had been or where they might be going.

"To Denver to start a bicycle repair shop," said Thelma as she pointed to a businessman with round glasses and a newspaper tucked under his arm.

"I think he's going to Albany to assassinate the governor."

"George! That is a downright awful thing to say," Thelma cried.

"Okay, he's a baseball scout, headed to Kansas City."

"Why Kansas City?" she asked.

"There are some great ballplayers from the Negro Leagues there. Now that Jackie Robinson is playing for the Dodgers, maybe more will get the chance."

"Maybe you should stop in Kansas City and pick up some ballplayers."

"Maybe I will." I pointed to a man dragging a long trunk. "Hot air balloon salesman."

"George, have you ever been in a balloon?"

"No, I haven't."

"I sure would like to go for a ride in one to see the world like a bird does. Promise me you'll take me for a balloon ride."

"I promise."

The public address announced my train. "George, you don't have to do this," Thelma pleaded. The realization that we would be apart until August caused her to doubt our decision to go along with her father's test. "We can come up with another plan."

"Your father is a stubborn man."

"So are you."

"That may be true, but I have to take this challenge."

"This isn't about winning my hand in marriage, is it? This is about you wanting to prove my father wrong."

"Maybe it is. I have spent the last five years on the inside watching the Yankees, Dodgers, and Giants run their clubs. I have ideas. I want to try something I've never done before."

Thelma looked into my eyes and paused. Shaking her head, she said, "You really are something, George Bennett. I believe in you. I just don't believe in a team that hasn't won in nineteen years."

"I guess that's a rational thing for a girl to think. But, don't give up on me. Even if we don't start winning right away."

"You had better get on the train." Thelma grabbed my neck and pulled me in for a long kiss.

"You're pretty forward for a socialite."

"And you're a good kisser for a Hoosier," she replied. "Call me. A lot."

"I will. A lot," I called back as I stepped on the train.

After settling in to my seat, I pulled out a new map I had purchased. "Surely a new map would have included Portis," I thought. Several minutes of study produced no evidence of the town. You can't find your life's destination on a map, and, apparently, you can't find Portis either. Maybe they're one and the same.

Why was Portis left off the map? Was it just lying around loose somewhere? Would I know it when I got there? Would the bus even stop in Portis? The concept of a town so small as to escape the watchful eyes of the Continental Map Company of East Rutherford, New Jersey, was too much for me to bear. So, I closed my eyes and drifted off to sleep.

I dreamt about being in elementary school and having to show the rest of the class a map of Kansas. "And this is Portis," I said. "The capital of Kansas."

"George Bennett, bring me your map this instant," barked the stone-faced teacher.

I lifted it off the easel and walked towards her desk. She snatched it out of my hands and held it close to her face. Then she lowered her glasses just enough to glare at me over the top of them.

"George Bennett, what's this?" she asked as she pulled away the paper I had pasted over Topeka. My plan was foiled. Unable to find anyone who knew where Portis was, I simply wrote Portis on a slip of paper and glued it over Topeka.

"George, do you know what we do with frauds at this school?"

"No," I answered.

"We make them clean erasers. Every day. For the rest of the year."

A whistle woke me up. I was out of the classroom and back in the train. We had stopped somewhere in Pennsylvania. I decided to take another look at that map.

~

When we arrived in Kansas City, I learned to my dismay that my luggage had disappeared. The clerk at the station told me that someone had helped themselves to several passengers' bags at the last stop. I had been sleeping and had no idea when my bag disappeared. Sitting in the station, I weighed my options. I could buy clothes now, or wait until I arrived in Portis.

"Sir, would you like a suitcase?"

I looked up to see the clerk standing before me. "Does it have clothes in my size in it?"

"No sir, but it's a start. Follow me."

I followed the clerk down a dimly lit hallway. The light fixtures shook as a train came in from Chicago. At the end of the hallway, he unlocked a red door with a sign that said, "Lost" in small black letters.

Inside this small closet, one could find years of history documented by the lost possessions of the American traveler. Travel bags sat on suitcases that rested on trunks. Coats for every season formed a mountain to the ceiling. Men's hats and women's hats and the lost toys of many children crammed their way into this little museum. Each artifact had settled here, despite its intended destination.

"This suitcase has been here for five years. I don't think anyone is coming back for it. Seeing how you're without one, why don't you take it?" offered the clerk.

"Thank you," I answered. I opened the brown leather case. Nothing was inside.

"I found it empty in the middle of the station," he continued.

"It will get the job done," I replied. "Thanks again." He gave me directions to a nearby Woolworth's where I could purchase a few things before I needed to be at the bus station. I didn't take the train to Portis because there were no seats available until the following day. The bus, I calculated, would get me there sooner.

I found the Woolworth's and the bus station easily. And with no other adventures to report, I fell asleep on the bus. When I woke up, I was in Portis.

Four

A portly fellow propped himself against the front wall of the post office. The building doubled also as a bus station and sat between Doc Burtch's office and Frank's Café. He wore a tattered blue hat with a frayed "P" that somewhat matched the blue of the jacket he wore. Next to him sat an empty Radio Flyer wagon. As the bus pulled to a stop, he straightened up and stepped towards the curb.

I lumbered down the aisle, past a half dozen inquisitive stares. When I stepped off the bus, the portly man stiffened up as if bracing for a punch.

"Are you Mr. Bennett?"

"Yes I am. Call me George," I offered my hand.

Timidly he shook it. After an awkward pause he said, "I'm Beanie. I mean Glen. I mean I am Glen Bush. But you can call me Glen or Beanie."

"Nice to meet you," I answered.

"I thought I would give you a tour of the town. You can put your things in this wagon," he said and nodded towards the Radio Flyer. I placed the worn suitcase in the wagon, even though it was nearly empty. He motioned down the street and began to pull the wagon. The lightness of the load made him glance back, then at me.

"You seem awful nervous. Are you okay?" I asked.

"Well, you're the new boss and I was hoping you would keep me on."

"You work for the Eskimos?"

"Yes, sir, seventeen years."

"What do you do?"

"I'm the equipment manager. Have been for 15 years. Took care of the grass before that…" he looked down at the ground. "You see, those boys who play for the team are like my sons. My wife and I couldn't have kids." He looked up at me and his lips began to tremble. "I'd do it for free, sir. The Eskimos are my family."

"I can promise you one more season. Anything after that is up to Mr. McClure. If we don't field a winning team, he may shut us down."

"I can't thank you enough," he said. He kept shaking my hand until my last comment sunk in. "But sir, these are the Eskimos. They haven't had a winning team in almost two decades."

"Why? Is it coaching, talent, or what?"

"Well, our local boys do their best I suppose. They play very hard, give it their all. However, I guess we are not growing many ballplayers here in Portis.

"How about the manager — is he any good?"

"The Eskimos don't have a manager, sir. He left after the season to sell insurance in Manhattan."

"New York, huh?"

"No, Manhattan, Kansas. We have a Manhattan, too. Of course theirs is an island," he said as if that was the only discernable difference between the two.

I stared at him for a moment, "Yeah, I'm sure other than Broadway, the skyscrapers, millions of people, and of course the island, they're a lot alike."

Beanie may have thought there was little difference between the two Manhattans, but even he couldn't compare Portis to New York. Portis, Kansas, is located on the Northern fork of the Solomon River. It originally was known as Bethany, Kansas, until the Central Branch Railroad sold out to the Missouri Pacific Railroad. This left the Missouri Pacific with the dilemma of having two Bethany stops along its route (Bethany, Missouri), which apparently in those days was simply unacceptable. So, Missouri Pacific did the only thing a sensible corporation could do in these situations and named one of the Bethanys after a company vice president (Mr. Portis).

Market Street (Highway 281) is the main thoroughfare of Portis, running north-south. The Missouri Pacific railroad tracks cut an east/west diagonal across the top of the town, while the Solomon River borders it to the south.

Two dozen or so buildings line Market Street, forming a commercial district. East/west roads cut across Market and provide the network of homes for Portis citizens. The ballpark sits north of town along the curve of Highway 281. Occasionally an opponent's home run would hit a car or roll across the highway and into the parking lot of the Honky Tonk Café.

Beanie concluded his guided tour and we stared at each other for an uncomfortable moment, then I inquired, "So, where is the rest of it?"

"The rest of what?"

"You know, the rest of the town."

"This is it. You've seen the whole town."

I looked back down Market Street. After a moment, I turned and looked the other way.

"Did you want me to show it to you again?"

I looked Beanie in the eyes. "No. No, I don't," I growled. Beanie looked hurt. He clutched the handle of his wagon tighter.

I stood in the middle of the street and studied the town for a few minutes I soaked in the buildings and the vast nothingness beyond. Beanie remained silent, though he fidgeted nervously. Finally, the sound of a car in the distance (the first one that had passed since I had been there) told me to move on to the sidewalk.

"So, where am I supposed to live?"

He pointed towards a store and started walking, "Mrs. Shaw runs the Five and Dime. She has rooms for you. Mr. McClure arranged it. He said the rent is coming out of your paycheck."

I shot him a look and he winced as if I was going to strike.

"Relax. I'm sorry I was sore at you. It's not your fault I'm in Portis. By the way, why is the team called the Eskimos?"

"That's on account of the Oquilluk brothers. They played outfield for the very first baseball team in Osborne County. "

"What's that got to do with Eskimos?"

"They weren't originally from here, you see. They were from Alaska. And, they were Eskimos. But they were bad at it."

"What do you mean?"

"Most Eskimos have a sort of sense about nature, direction, living off the land and all that. These boys didn't have none of that stuff. Took off one winter with their dog sleds to join a seal hunt, wound up in Kansas."

"You mean to tell me they drove dog sleds from Alaska

to Kansas?"

"No, the dogs died somewhere in Montana. They claim they rode buffaloes the rest of the way, but I don't believe it."

"And they stayed in Kansas?"

"They weren't all that sure how to get back." He paused to motion to the store, "here we are."

We knocked on the front door of the Five and Dime. They had long since closed for the day, but Beanie had arranged for me to meet Mrs. Shaw.

"You should knock harder."

I hit the door a few more times. "Harder."

"I don't want to knock the door down," I said as I hit it again.

"You see, the thing is, she's hard of hearing."

Just then, the door swung open and a woman dressed like the very first settler to arrive in the majestic state of Kansas shouted, "Why are you knocking so loud? Do you think I am deaf?"

No, but I think I am now, I thought to myself. "Hi, I'm George Bennett," I said. "I'm here about the room."

"I know why you're here. Follow me," she shouted.

The power in her voice knocked me against the wall and Beanie against the doorframe. She brushed past us, out the door, and disappeared to the right. Stepping out, we realized she was already around the corner. We followed to the alley where she had covered most of the length of the building and was preparing to climb steps to a small landing on the second floor.

"She's like a cat," I said to Beanie.

"Hurry up," she called back.

At the top of the stairs, we entered a small, furnished apartment. It had a bedroom, a bathroom, and a kitchen-living-dining room combination. I say combo in the sense that the oven door, when open, served as the coffee table in front of the couch.

"You want me to get rid of the whore?" shouted Mrs. Shaw.

"Excuse me?"

"The whore behind you."

 I looked back out the door and then down the steps.

"What whore?"

"That whore," she yelled, then pushed the door shut and pulled me into the kitchen-living-dining room. That is when I saw the whore. I mean woman. I mean, that is when I saw the large picture of Lana Turner.

"Last fellow to live here left it. But you don't look like the kind of a man who would have a whore on his wall." She looked me up and down.

"No ma'am, I…"

"Of course, neither did he," she paused and squinted at me. "Maybe you do want the whore on your wall?"

"No. No, ma'am. I don't want the whore on my wall. I mean, I don't think Lana is a whore but…"

"Look at her," she shouted. "Bosoms nearly falling out of that dress. Wearing enough makeup to paint a school."

"Paint a school? What does that mean? Look all I'm trying to say is…"

"Maybe I just don't need another man looking at whores above my Five and Dime." She shook her head and crossed her arms.

"Ma'am, I would be happy if you removed the whore — um, picture from this apartment."

Satisfied with my answer, she reached to take it down. She pulled with all of her 90-pound frame's strength, but it would not budge. Beanie and I pulled and it did not move. Upon closer inspection, we observed that it had been screwed in to the wall.

"Now, I remember why I hadn't moved it before. Well, here is the key," she yelled as she dropped the key in my hand. "I'll be back tomorrow for the whore."

"Yes, ma'am. Goodnight."

"Do you need anything, sir?" Beanie asked.

"No, thanks. But please, call me George. I'll see you tomorrow."

Beanie took one last long look at Lana. Then Mrs. Shaw grabbed him by the ear and pulled him outside. With her other hand, she grabbed the doorknob, shouting, "whore" as the door pulled shut.

I sat down and looked around the apartment. Like it or not, I was in Portis, and this was my home. After unpacking, I called Thelma to tell her I had arrived safely. After a brief conversation, I walked to the bedroom, pausing to turn off the light. "Good night, Lana." I flicked the switch and heard what sounded like Thelma's voice coming from the picture, "Good night."

I turned the light on but no one was there. I stared at the picture and listened. Confident that I had imagined it, I turned the light off and went to sleep.

~

Beanie knocked on the door the next morning. I was awake and dressed, ready to start the quest to win Thelma.

"Good morning," said Beanie. "Thought you might want to go to breakfast at Frank's."

"Sure, that sounds swell," I answered. I waved goodbye to Lana, pulled the door shut, and followed Beanie down the rickety metal stairs. Before reaching the bottom, I noticed the return of the Radio Flyer. When we reached the bottom, Beanie grabbed the handle and pulled it behind him. The wagon carried a large burlap sack. Several wooden bat handles were sticking out of the bag.

"Why are you..." I started to ask, and then decided it could wait until I had a full stomach. However, I was beginning to suspect he took the wagon everywhere he went. Beanie glanced back, but kept walking.

I followed him out of the alley and past several buildings. When we arrived at Frank's Café, the town, and I mean the whole town, was crammed in to see the new fellow. People were squeezed in booths and standing around filled tables. The ones that couldn't get in were standing around the benches in front of the restaurant pretending not to stare through the window. Only two seats remained empty.

"Sit there," Beanie pointed to a seat next to a tall skinny fellow. Both men at the table rose and extended their hands.

"I'm Pastor Willoughby, of the First United Church of the MethoBaptists," said the tall skinny fellow.

"The first church of what?"

"We're the First United Church of the MethoBaptists," he said proudly. "And when I say first, I really mean first. We're the first church in the entire state of Kansas to unite the Baptists with the Methodists. We might even be the first in the country, although we haven't confirmed that."

Beanie nodded his head to confirm Pastor Willoughby's declaration. "Alice Simpson, our beloved organist and church historian is looking into it as we speak," the pastor said.

"Well, I hope she comes back with good news," I answered. "I know I never heard of such a church."

Pastor Willoughby looked over his shoulder to the crowd. "I knew he would be a fine addition to the community." He turned back to me, "And what church do you attend, brother?"

"In New York, I attended a Lutheran congregation. We tried to merge with the Greek Orthodox Church, but we couldn't agree on what hats to wear."

This attempt at humor caused Pastor Willoughby to doubt his

earlier assessment of my character. I didn't have time to follow up because the mayor grabbed my hand. "I'm Mayor Griffin," he said while he continued to shake my hand. Quite vigorously, I might add.

"I want to welcome you to Portis."

"Thank you," I replied. "So far, everyone has been quite friendly."

"Do you still have the whore in your apartment?" shouted the surprisingly-powerful-for-this-time-in-the-morning voice of Mrs. Shaw.

Everyone gasped and looked at me. I turned to Beanie and muttered, "Except her."

I looked around Frank's Café and everyone silently waited for me to explain the whore. "Umm, Mrs. Shaw's former tenant left a picture of Lana Turner permanently stuck to the wall. We haven't been able to remove the whore — I mean, picture."

After some mumbling and discussion, it seemed everyone was okay with this explanation. When it was evident that I wasn't going to be run out of town, the mayor raised his glass of orange juice and proclaimed, "Welcome to the new general manager of the Eskimos and the co-manager of McClure's Agricultural Products."

I had almost forgotten McClure had saddled me with helping run the store. What did I know about seed and fertilizer? As a journalist, I did know how to spread the manure, so to speak, so maybe it wouldn't be that hard.

The crowd cheered and clapped and generally welcomed me to Portis, except for the pastor, who kept an eye on me, and Mrs. Shaw, who left Frank's Café flailing her arms and shouting about whores.

A harried, young waitress took our order. After a pleasant breakfast with an enthusiastic mayor and a suspicious pastor, we excused ourselves and walked outside. There, to my New York amazement, was Beanie's Radio Flyer. Untouched.

"Nobody ran off with your stuff."

"Why would somebody do that?" he asked. The possibility did not even occur to these people.

"We're not in New York anymore," I said.

"I've never been there, sir."

"I know," I said. "I was just making a play on a famous movie line." I could see he was not getting it. "Oh, forget it. Let's go to work."

∼

Beanie and I walked to the grain elevator. McClure's Agricultural Products was attached, along with a shed to hold the baseball equipment. In addition to being the equipment manager, Beanie ran the shop. I would have to co-manage with him for the summer, but as far as I was concerned, when it came to farming, he would be the boss.

We entered the store and were welcomed by Morton Slinkard. Morton, or Mort as he liked to be called, was in his late twenties. He loved baseball and knew every nuance of the game. Folks say he hit like Stan Musial, but he had suffered an injury serving his country during World War II. A mortar shell ripped through his leg on D-Day. Doctors saved his leg, but he would forever walk with a limp and watch the game from the dugout.

Beanie pointed to a door and said, "That's your office, sir. Have a look while I go over this order with Mort."

I looked around the shop first, then opened the door to my first private office. I surveyed the layout and leaned back into the store. "Beanie, my office looks a lot like the men's bathroom."

"That's on account of it being the men's bathroom."

"You don't say."

"Yes sir, we don't have but two offices. You're welcome to the other if you don't want to be in the bathroom."

"Let me guess — the women's bathroom?"

"No sir, it's a closet." He opened the door to reveal a tiny closet. A wooden shelf served as a desk. A pin-up girl calendar and clippings from the Portis Independent lined the wall. A filing cabinet and a phone sat outside the door.

"I'm not a fan of small places, so I'll take the bathroom," I said.

"That sure is a relief sir. I really didn't want to have to move all my stuff."

I looked at the closet and then looked at Beanie. Best not to ask, I thought, and retreated into my new office. I sat down at my desk and took inventory. I had a phone and a filing cabinet. Directly in front of me was a sink. To my left were a stall and a floor length urinal. It was nothing like the offices at Yankee stadium. My office made me realize just how far away from the big leagues I had traveled.

$\sim$

That afternoon we took in the Eskimos' first practice of the season. Sixteen would-be ballplayers were playing catch when we arrived. Some were well into their forties while others looked like children.

"Beanie, some of those guys look like they're in high school."

"They are. The school doesn't have a team, so they play for the Eskimos."

"What about that guy? He looks like he's fifty."

"No, Lester's only forty-six. He just looks that way 'cause of hard living."

"What position does he play?"

"First base. Lester has been playing first for the Eskimos for nineteen years," he said with pride.

"And that is how long you have gone without a winning season."

Beanie looked at Lester and then back at me. "Huh," he grunted then walked into the middle of the players.

"All right, gather 'round." Everyone complied except for a young man leaning against a girl out in left field. "Turner! Stop kissing that girl and get in here. Sally, what are you doing here? You know there ain't no game today."

When Turner joined the group, he kneeled sheepishly in the back. Beanie glared at him for a moment. "Boys, this is Mr. Bennett. You all know Mr. McClure has sent him to run the Eskimos this summer." Most of them nodded and looked at me suspiciously. "I'm going to stay on as coach and Mort will still be helping out."

"What about a manager?" Lester asked.

"I haven't hired a manager yet," I said.

"Why not?" asked Lester. "The season starts in a month."

Beanie jumped in to save me, "Now boys, he hasn't even been in town for a full day. Let's give him some time to settle in."

I nodded to Beanie, who told the players to take batting practice. I sat down in the bleachers and took notes. Beanie seemed to know his way around the diamond, dispensing skill lessons here and disciplining the unfocused there. Maybe he could make a good manager, I thought. The players seemed to respond to him.

It suddenly occurred to me that Beanie, Mort, and I were here. Who was running the store? "Beanie, what about the store? Shouldn't one of us be there?"

"Why, Mr. Bennett?" said Beanie.

"Please call me George. What if a customer comes," I asked.

Mort and Beanie laughed. "Who would come while we are at practice?" Beanie said.

I obviously was missing some key information that Beanie was about to supply. "Folks in town know to do their business before practice. Most of the farmers around town keep our schedule in their barns so they know when to shop. So relax, we're not losing any business."

This was definitely Kansas. And, after about a half hour of practice, I knew why this was the K.R.A.P. League. Turner and a guy that everyone called Sweets seemed to be the only ones with above average talent. Maybe good enough for high AA ball. The rest were bushers — not much better than the below-average high school player.

Beanie came up to the bleachers and leaned on the fence. His back was to me so he could continue monitoring the players. "So, what do you think?" he asked.

"We've got a lot of work to do."

"Yes, but I think we can climb out of last place this year. Maybe finish as high as eighth."

"That's not good enough. We have to win the pennant."

Beanie turned around. "I know you said that last night, but you're never going to do it with these guys."

"I can see that. We need to start scouting for players."

"We have the best players in Portis."

Beanie sensed that his answer didn't make me feel better. We both stared at the players and the field for a while. I stood and looked in every direction. My mission seemed hopeless. Then I looked at the field again. This time I noticed irregularities in the grass. I walked to the top bleacher and surveyed the field.

"Beanie, why does the field look like a patchwork quilt?"

"That's on account of the 4-H Kids."

"How's that?"

"The 4-H kids maintain the field. Each kid has a 20-by-20 plot in the outfield to take care of and most of them are using different types of grass."

"Please be kidding."

"I'm serious sir. They take a lot of pride in it."

"What about that plot in right field? It's just a big square of mud with a weed in the center."

"The boy responsible for that one is a little strange."

"Really? What's his name?"

"Mudd. Billy Mudd."

"Well, that's ironic, don't you think?"

"No sir, I believe his folks are German."

Five

After practice, I walked home to my apartment. The phone was ringing when I entered. "Hello," I said.

"Bennett, where have you been? I've been ringing you for an hour," said the gruff voice of Hubert McClure.

"I was at practice, sir."

"How does the team look?" he said with a chuckle.

"Great, sir," I lied. "We should easily finish ten games ahead of Red Cloud."

"What?" he screamed. "That bunch of plowboys couldn't beat a team of Girl Scouts."

"Thank you for your confidence, sir. I will be sure to pass along your good wishes to the team."

"My pleasure, Bennett. Now, the reason I called is that I have been looking at your books. We are going to have to make some cutbacks."

"Sir, we already have 4-H kids doing the groundskeeping. How much more can you cut back?"

"Well, I'm afraid you won't have the money to hire a manager."

"Sir, you can't take away the money for a manager. How am I supposed to compete without a manager?"

"I thought you said they were good enough to finish ten games ahead of Red Cloud? I am sorry, Bennett. One of the assistants can manage or you can do it.

"Well, how much money are you giving me to work with?"

"$1,200 per month."

"I'm supposed to pay Beanie, Mort, and the players on $1,200 per month?

"And yourself."

"That's ridiculous! How can I run a team on that amount of money?"

"If you want to marry my daughter, I guess you will just have to find a way. Goodnight."

He hung up on me before I could plead my case any further. Well, at least I could add four more players to the roster. "Can you believe this?" I asked Lana. She didn't answer.

I considered my options and decided it made the most sense to let Beanie manage. At least that way I could focus on finding players. The next morning, I called Beanie into my office.

"Beanie, I have been thinking. It might be time for you to think about passing the equipment manager's job to Mort."

"But sir, I…" Beanie started to panic.

"Hold on now, just hear me out. You know this team as well as anybody and have watched more baseball than any other man in Portis. I think you should be the manager."

"Are you serious?"

"Yes, I am. With you managing, I can focus on getting us some ballplayers. Is it a deal?"

"Absolutely! You won't regret this, George!" It was the first time he called me George without prompting.

"Good, now go get Mort."

"I'm in here, sir." Mort had been sitting in the stall the entire time.

"Mort, I need you to be equipment manager and coach first base. I will be handling the scouting and coach third. You already know that Beanie is going to manage. What do you say to that?"

"I'm much obliged, sir," he answered before flushing.

"Good, now let's go take inventory."

Beanie and Mort followed me single file into the equipment room. "What kind of shape are the uniforms in?"

Beanie replied, "The road jerseys are in good shape, but the home uniforms are falling apart. He pulled random jerseys and pants out of a box. Most had holes or mold damage.

"Most of this stuff was damaged in the off-season," Mort explained. "A tree limb crashed through the roof and let the rain and snow in all winter. Nobody had a reason to go in here during the off-season, so we didn't find it until February."

"Any place in town where we could get new jerseys or at least repair the ones we have?"

"Riddle's Department Store could repair them. There is a place in Kansas City that supplies most of the teams in the league. Might take them a while, though."

"What about the rest of the equipment?"

"We have two dozen bats that are still usable. Wolter's Lumber Yard makes us new ones when we need them. Plenty of practice balls are in here, but we only have a dozen game balls. We will have to order more to get through the season. Catcher's equipment is in good shape. I would say we could get by with just ordering game balls, home uniforms and hats. Of course, if you're writing down a wish list, a new third base would be nice."

"Third base? What's wrong with third base?"

"It's red."

"Red?"

"Yes, sir," answered Mort. "Third base is red."

Turning to Beanie in hopes of a more elaborate answer, I asked, "Why is third base red?"

"A few years ago, Inez Walker, the town gossip, told Henry Harrison's wife that he had been seen holding hands and heaven only knows what with a woman in the bleachers at the Igloo," said Beanie.

"What's the Igloo?"

"Folks round here call the park where the Eskimos play the Igloo."

I stared in disbelief. "Okay, but how did the base get red?"

"Well, Henry played third base for the Eskimos. When Mrs. Harrison found out, she set fire to the bleachers and painted third base red. We think she might have been gassed."

"Clearly. But why red?"

"Because the woman with Henry— a beautician-in-training— was a redhead and that very morning, before Inez spilled the beans, Henry had made the unfortunate suggestion that his wife color her hair red."

"So, why don't you paint it back?"

"We did. But, every year on the anniversary of the indiscretion, she gets drunk and paints it back. After last year, we gave up. The guys complained about the multiple layers of paint on the base."

"All right," I answered. "I'll keep my eyes open for another base."

Six

When I got to the office the next morning, I called Thelma. She didn't recognize my voice at first. "It's me, George."

"Your voice sounds different. Kind of like an echo."

"I'm in a bathroom."

"George Bennett! Have you gone to the Midwest and lost all sense of decency? How dare you call me from a public restroom?"

"It's not a public restroom. It's my office."

"This is no time for crass jokes."

"No, I'm serious. My office is in the men's bathroom. And, I might remind you, this place belongs to your father. He is the reason my desk is five feet from a urinal."

"Oh. Then I'm sorry I was cross with you. How does the team look?"

"Beanie says they're better than last year."

"Are they good enough to beat Red Cloud?"

"I haven't seen Red Cloud play. But, if they are as good as everyone says, we don't have a chance. In fact, I don't think we could beat a team that had my mom pitching."

"This is not encouraging news, George Bennett."

"Neither is the fact that your father is cutting back on our payroll. I only have enough money to pay three employees and that includes me. I'm sorry; I'm going to have to cut our talk short. There seems to be a commotion outside."

"Okay, call me again soon. I love you."

"I will, and I love you, too. Goodbye."

I was irritated that I had to cut the call short. However, I could hear an argument getting louder outside. I ran out the front door to find Mort and Beanie scuffling on the ground.

"It's always been mine," growled Beanie.

"But I'm the equipment manager now," snapped Mort.

"What are you guys fighting about?" I asked.

Beanie freed himself from Mort and stood up. "Sir, he's trying to take the…" Mort pulled Beanie back to the ground. "… the Radio Flyer."

"You guys are fighting over the wagon?"

"It's mine," Beanie said.

"Not any more," said Mort.

"Beanie," I said, "is this any way for a manager to behave?"

Beanie let go of Mort, stood up and dusted himself off. Mort stared at the ground, sensing that they were in trouble. Beanie sheepishly explained, "But I've always pulled the wagon."

"I know, but you're the manager now. It's time for Mort to have it."

Mort's face lit up, and then he quickly looked back at the ground in case the scolding wasn't finished.

I walked over to the wagon, took the handle and pulled it over to

Beanie. "Now, pass the handle over to Mort."

Slowly he handed it over. "There now," I said to Beanie. "Don't you feel better?"

"No."

"Well, you will after a while," I said.

Beanie mumbled to himself and went back inside. I slapped Mort on the back of his head.

"Hey, what did you do that for?"

"He's an old man. You could have hurt him," I chided.

"I'm the equipment manager and this is part of the equipment," he protested.

The next day I arrived to find a shiny new Radio Flyer parked in front of the store. A clipboard, line-up cards and a pair of spikes filled the wagon.

"Went out and bought a new wagon, didn't you?" I asked Beanie.

"Yep," was all said.

I shook my head and went to my office. Someone was sitting in the stall singing "Mack the Knife." I decided to make coffee.

~

Later that day, Mort returned from lunch in a panic. "Beanie, Mr. Bennett, we have a big problem."

"What now," I asked.

"It's Turner."

"Yeah, what is it?" asked Beanie.

"Sally's pregnant."

"Who's Sally?" I asked.

"She works the scoreboard for us," Beanie replied. "Don't you remember her from the first day of practice?"

"Oh, I remember. You got on Turner for paying more attention to her than the practice," I said. "How far along is she?"

"Six months," said Mort.

"Six months? You can't even tell," I exclaimed.

"Well, apparently she is starting to show, now," Mort said.

"That means she's liable to have the kid during the season," I said.

"That's not even the worst part. She just happens to be Don Riddle's daughter," added Mort.

"As in Riddle's Department Store," said Beanie.

"Do you think that will be a problem?" I asked.

"Well, we could wear the road uniforms at home, but we have no hats," Beanie explained.

Mort piled on, "League rules say that all players must wear a hat."

I rolled my eyes. "Thanks, Mort. Maybe you should run to the shop and see if you can get our uniforms before Mr. Riddle finds out he is going to be a grandfather."

"Yes, sir," said Mort.

"Oh, and one more thing. Tell Turner we want to see him right now."

Turner knocked on the door a few minutes later. "You wanted to see me?"

"The scoreboard operator? What the hell were you thinking?" I asked.

Beanie threw a ball at him. It missed and hit the Tractor of the Month calendar.

"Does this mean I'm off the team?"

"No, it means you're out of the dugout," I said. "You are keeping score from now on. I can't have a pregnant woman out there in that heat."

"Does her family know?" I asked.

"Yes, sir," Turner answered.

"You better hope we get those uniforms or you're playing in a dress," Beanie shouted.

"Do you plan on marrying this girl?" I asked.

"I'm only nineteen."

"And she's only eighteen," yelled Beanie.

"Are you scared?" I asked.

"Yes, sir."

"That might be a good thing," I said. "It will help you pay better attention."

"Pay attention to what, sir?"

"The world. Your finances. What you do. What you say," I said. "You have three people to think about now. Not just yourself."

Beanie added, "You are going to need a new job and a place to live."

Tears welled up in Turner's eyes. "I didn't think about that," he muttered. Then he walked silently out of the office with his head down.

Beanie motioned towards the door and said, "Should I..."

"Go take care of him," I said. "I'll hold down the fort."

Without even stopping to grab his wagon, Beanie hurried to catch Turner.

~

Mort returned later with the bad news. "Mr. Riddle is quite sore about his daughter."

"And?"

"He's not going to make the new uniforms."

"How long will it take the guy in Kansas City?"

"Four and a half weeks."

"How many games is that?"

"Eight. Plus whatever preseason games you had scheduled."

"Okay, I'll call the other teams and tell them we're wearing our road uniforms for a while."

"What about hats?"

"Check every store in town. Don't come back without twenty matching hats."

Later that afternoon, Mort returned with two large boxes. He quickly set them on the desk and backed away as if to avoid being hit.

"What did you find?" I asked.

"There are only two stores in the greater Portis area that have twenty identical hats," Mort said.

"Okay, so what are our choices?"

He approached the desk slowly and opened both boxes. "Our first option"—he reached into the first box and pulled out a woman's bonnet—"is this stylish hat from Madam Kirkpatrick's Boutique."

He put it on and stared at me as if he actually needed me to say we were not going to wear them. I looked at Beanie and he shrugged his shoulders as if to say, "I can live with it."

I shook my head and looked back at Mort. "What is in box Number Two?"

He took off the bonnet, reached into the box and pulled out a green Army helmet. He put it on and pleaded with his eyes.

I nodded and said, "Helmets."

Mort sighed and closed the box of bonnets quickly in case I changed my mind. Then he handed Beanie a helmet. He put it on and said, "It's not so bad."

"Yes, it is," I answered.

Even though they looked ridiculous, I knew that the helmets were the least of our worries. We needed ballplayers. I had to start recruiting outside of Portis. It was time for a road trip.

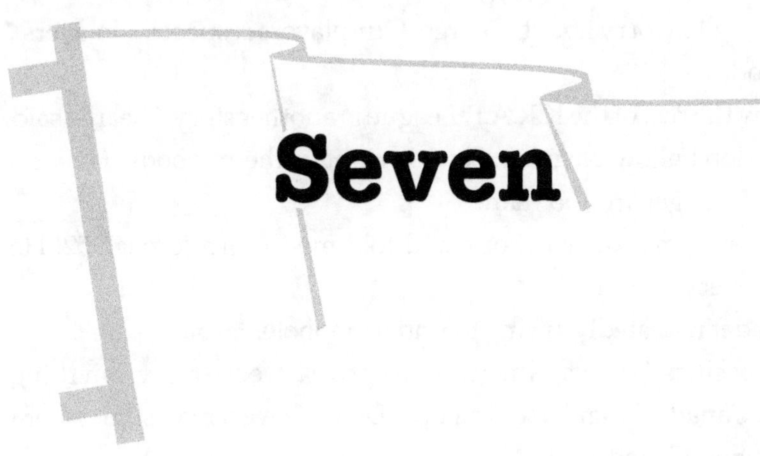

Seven

On Monday, I announced to Beanie and Mort that I would be out of town for a few days.

"Beanie, I'm going to Kansas City to get a ballplayer that could help the team. I'm just a little concerned about something."

"What is it," he said.

"How do folks around here feel about colored folk?"

Beanie's eyes flashed with excitement, and he said, "You're going to get somebody from the Negro Leagues."

"Yes, I am. But, will the people of Portis accept him?"

"I suspect they will," Beanie said. "There might be a few people that don't take to him, but not many."

"What about the guys on the team?"

"No problems there," Beanie said. "Heck, we all went to see one of them colored teams play Moonlight a few years ago. We were the only white folk cheering against the Sonatas. No, you don't have anything to worry about, George. Our players respect ballplayers."

"Good."

"Now the rest of the K.R.A.P. League is another story," Beanie said. "They don't allow Negroes. Says so right in the rulebook. How do you plan to get around that?"

He tossed me the rulebook and told me to turn to page 52. He knew every word in it.

I read it repeatedly, trying to find a loophole.

"It specifically says American Negroes. Doesn't say anything about Canada," I said, looking up. "Do we have a map somewhere that shows Canada?"

"I think so," Beanie said. He fumbled through some drawers until he produced a map. I studied it for a few minutes until I decided on a town.

"Beanie, we're going to start bringing in players from Kamloops."

"Where?"

"Exactly. If you've never heard of it, most likely no one else has either."

"Are you going up there to scout? I don't even think they have a league."

"No, you're missing the point," I said. "I'm going to tell the league that our new player is from Kamloops, in Canada."

"Are you sure you can sign this guy?"

"I'm pretty sure."

Ray Robinson played the guitar well enough to scratch out a living. He played baseball well enough to play professionally. The only thing he lacked was a set of white parents. Since his baseball skills were just shy of being good enough to remain in the Negro

National League and no white minor leagues would have him, he played guitar.

I met Ray in New York where he spent one season as a backup outfielder for the New York Cubans. We kept in touch after he moved to Kansas City. That proved to be a wise decision because the Eskimos needed help. The K.R.A.P. league was about to be integrated.

I got off the bus in a part of Kansas City that was not accustomed to seeing white folks all too often. A man waiting for the next bus asked me, "You sure you got off at the right stop?"

"I'm pretty sure. Do you know Ray Robinson?"

"Sure, everybody in this neighborhood knows Ray."

"Does he still play guitar at the Blue Moon Tavern?"

He grinned and replied, "Five nights a week." He looked me up and down. "What do you want with Ray," he asked in a suspicious tone.

"I'm an old friend from his baseball days."

"You wouldn't happen to be that white reporter who used to come to the colored baseball games, would you? Ray talks about you all the time."

"I sure am. Do you know where he might be right now?" I asked.

"He's probably over at the tavern — practicing for tonight."

The old man gave me directions to the Blue Moon. When I walked in, two of the three men sitting at the bar spit out whatever they were drinking. The spray covered the bartender. Towards the back, a lone musician sat tuning his guitar on an otherwise empty stage. His back was to me.

"You play that thing like you hit," I said.

"And how might that be," he asked without turning around.

The men at the bar waited, silently, for my reply.

"Pretty lousy in practice. But you do okay when a crowd is in the house."

The three old men gasped, expecting the musician to hit me over the head with his guitar.

"Yeah, well you write like you drink," he replied.

"And how might that be?"

"Don't matter which one you're doing, somebody's going to have to clean up a mess."

The three men and the bartender howled with laughter.

"Ray Robinson."

"George Bennett," he replied. Then he sat down his guitar and turned to face me. Then we both laughed and hugged.

"George, what on earth are you doing in Kansas City?"

"I'm scouting talent."

"You lookin' for musicians?"

"No, I'm looking for ballplayers."

"Ballplayers? What happened to the sports writing? Did they get tired of you writing about the Negro League? I told you that was going to get you into trouble."

"No, I didn't get fired. I sort of got reassigned. I'm running a baseball team this summer. It's sort of a challenge."

"Running a baseball team, huh? Well, I suppose you could succeed at that. Always did know the game better than most of the folks writing for the paper."

"I will never succeed without more talent. Ray, would you consider playing in the K.R.A.P. league?"

"I don't know George, I got a steady playing gig here."

"Come on, Ray. You can't tell me that you wouldn't want one more chance to play ball every day. You still have a few good years left in you."

"Maybe I do, maybe I don't. But they don't allow no coloreds in that league."

"I think I have a way around that. Do you have any objection to telling people you are Canadian?"

"How much does it pay?"

"Five dollars a week plus a room for the baseball season, and we can get you a job somewhere else to make ends meet."

"George, I'm making more than that here."

"How much more?"

"Well, the Kansas City music scene ain't what it was when I was a just a kid startin' out. Did you know I snuck in to the Reno Club back in 1935? I heard Basie and the Barons of Rhythm that night. This used to be a great town for jazz and blues musicians."

"How much?"

"I figure I bring in forty bucks a week with tips."

"Okay, I'll match that plus the room and board. But, I'm going to have to take a pay cut."

"You must really want me to play. What's the catch?"

"No catch. I just need this team to win the league pennant."

"Are they any good?"

"Haven't had a winning season in 19 years."

"You want me to go all the way to Nowhere, Kansas, to play for team that is on a 20-year losing streak?"

"Nineteen."

"Nineteen, whatever. George you're crazy. This ain't even an affiliated league. It's not like some scout for the St. Louis Cardinals is going to stumble across me in Podunk."

"Portis."

"Whatever the name is, I'm not going."

"I know you like playing the guitar, but you have your whole life to sit on that stool. You only have a couple of years left to play baseball. If you pass this chance up, you will regret it."

"For years, white people didn't want my kind in the game. Now here you are beggin' me to play."

"It wasn't me that kept you out. Come on, I was the only white reporter to cover your games in New York."

"Yeah, I know. It's just funny how things turn out. Stay for the show tonight. I'll think about it while I play. Music has a way of helping me think clearer."

~

The next morning I met Ray for breakfast.

"You said something last night about Canada," Ray asked.

"I found a loophole in the rulebook. It specifically states that American blacks are not allowed," I said.

"So, what am I?"

"As far as the league office is concerned, you would be Canadian."

"Do I have to speak Canadian?"

"Not if you don't want to," I assured him.

"Whew! Well then, I'm obliged to you. I thought about what you said. My daddy's dream was to see me break the color barrier and play ball with the white folks. Of course, I wasn't quite good enough and Jackie got there first. But, playing in this league is sort of a first. So, I want to do this for my dad."

He offered his hand and we shook on the deal. I had my centerfielder. Now I needed a pitcher.

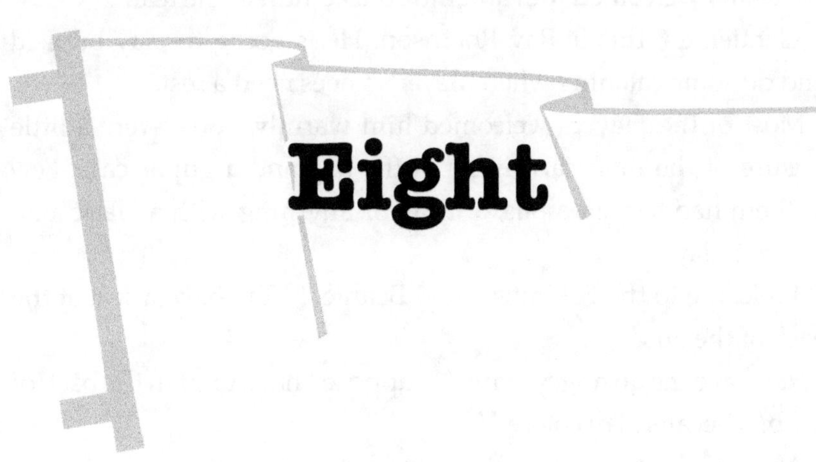

Eight

A few days later, we were ready for our first road trip. I had scheduled exhibition games in Amarillo, Texas; Roswell, New Mexico, and a few towns in between. I wanted to see how we played against real competition, but do it far away enough from Kansas so nobody caught wind of our Canadian ballplayer. I also hoped the 1200 mile round trip would bring the team together.

Mort and I were outside the team bus, waiting for Ray to arrive in town. We were trying to cram a red wagon into the already loaded baggage compartment. I decided to pull my suitcase out to make room for the Radio Flyer. The borrowed luggage had been given a splash of color: Mort had painted a giant "P" on the side to match our uniforms.

Since Ray's bus was late, he practically jumped from one bus to the next. I welcomed him and introduced him to the team.

"Gentlemen, this is Ray Robinson. He is going to play outfield and do some catching when Meyer's knees need a rest."

Most of the players welcomed him warmly. Some were a little unsure of the man carrying a duffle bag and a guitar case. Few of them had shared a bus, a meal, or anything with a black man before today.

"Welcome to the Eskimos," said Beanie. "Now have a seat at the back of the bus."

Ray gave me an angry stare. "I suppose I have to sit in the back of the bus because I'm colored."

"No, you have to sit in the back of the bus because you're an outfielder," I said quickly.

"Huh?"

"It's how everybody is sitting," I explained. "Pitchers in the front, infield in the middle, and all the outfielders are in the back."

He studied the layout. Since he had just joined the team, he didn't know if we were telling the truth or were really trying to relegate him to the back. I nodded to reassure him, then smiled wide. "How about that?"

He took his seat with the outfielders. By the time we left the county, he was playing his guitar. Surprisingly, that summer we didn't have problems amongst the players. The Eskimos did not worry about color, or politics, or what church you went to on Sunday. After nineteen losing seasons, these guys would play with a Martian if it meant winning a few more games.

～

After we won our game in Amarillo courtesy of a one-run error, we decided to celebrate by picking up some Chinese food before leaving town. The cook came out of the kitchen as soon as he heard there was a baseball team ordering carry-out.

"Are you men with the baseball team?"

"Yes, I'm George Bennett and this is our manager, Beanie."

"I was wondering if you needed a lefty in your rotation," he said.

"How much experience have you had," I asked.

"I made it as far as Sacramento in the Pacific Coast League. That was in 1941. I had a good summer — struck out ninety-three. Then the Japanese bombed Pearl Harbor and there was no playing after that. Nobody wanted me on their team."

"You Japanese?" asked Beanie.

"Korean."

"And you work in a Chinese restaurant?"

"You people can't tell the difference," the cook said.

"Well, you got me there," I answered. "Tell you what; I noticed a field behind this restaurant when we pulled into town. Be back there in ten minutes and we'll give you a look."

"Yes, sir," he smiled and ran back to the kitchen.

"What about the food?" said Beanie.

"Have Mort take care of it." I gave him some cash and went back to the bus.

"Ray," I shouted.

"What, coach?"

"Grab a bat and come with me. We're giving another Canadian a tryout."

He smiled at the other players. "Two of us. Well, there goes the neighborhood."

Ray, Beanie and I found the chef waiting for us in the small field behind the restaurant.

"I thought you said he was black," said Ray.

"No, I said he was Canadian."

"But on this team, Canadian means black."

"Let's decide after we see him pitch." I was hungry and tired, so I did not want to argue. I did, however, need a pitcher. I did not believe he had pitched for the Sacramento Solons, but I had to be sure.

"Okay, Ray is going to stand in. Beanie will catch. Do you need a few warm-ups?"

"I'll take a few," the cook said. He proceeded to throw strike after strike. Each one came in harder than the last. After several throws, Beanie called for a curve. It started high towards an imaginary batter's head, and then darted low and to the opposite corner of the plate. Beanie looked at me and smiled.

"Step in, Ray."

Ray stepped in and flailed at pitch after pitch. Fastballs, sliders, curves and change-ups. The chef could not be hit.

"What do you think, Ray?" I asked.

"I once faced Satchel Paige, 'bout ten years ago. They're neck and neck sir."

"Is he Canadian?"

Ray smiled wide. "Soon as I teach him the anthem."

"Good." I turned to the chef. "What did you say your name was?"

"Bobby Park."

"Bobby?" Beanie and I asked.

"Yeah, my parents wanted me to have an American name."

"Prejudice drove you out of the game seven years ago," I said. "Can you handle it if folks give you a hard time now?"

"I can take it from the fans, but not my teammates." He paused and looked me in the eyes. "I've got to know now if they are going to accept me."

I put my arm around his shoulder to reassure him. "Bobby, I think you'll find that this group of guys is willing to accept anybody in order to win. Where did you say you were from?"

"San Francisco."

"Really? Have you ever been to Canada?"

~

That very day, Korean Bobby Park quit his job making Chinese food in Amarillo, Texas, to pitch for the Portis Eskimos. But first, he would have to travel to Roswell.

"Where in tarnation is Roswell, New Mexico," asked Mort as we left Amarillo.

"It's about a half day's drive from here," said Bobby.

"We're playing an exhibition against Roswell's minor league team," I added.

Beanie wrinkled his brow. "Hey, isn't that where the spaceship landed last year," he asked.

"Yeah, they said it crashed there and the government has the ship. I've even heard they captured an alien," Bobby declared.

The previous July, the Roswell Daily Record reported that the United States government had captured a UFO on a ranch near Roswell, New Mexico. Initially, the Roswell Army Airfield had reported the crash of a flying disc. Later that same day, the commanding general of the Eighth Air Force declared it was a weather balloon.

Since the two reports conflicted, folks were suspicious of the government's response — thinking that Uncle Sam must be covering something up. Some even believed that little green men might be lurking around Roswell.

Later that afternoon, Beanie and I were discussing the lineup on the road to Roswell when Mort interrupted us. "Sir, Sweets has been acting weird all day. He keeps mumbling something about getting revenge and somebody named Alice," he warned.

I looked at Beanie and asked, "Do you want to take this one or should I?"

"You handle Sweets. I want to work on a lineup for tomorrow."

"Alright."

I slid into the seat next to Sweets. "How are you doing," I offered.

He looked at me for a while, studying my face. Then he asked, "You ever had someone take your girl?"

"Yes, it happened to me in high school."

"Well, he took my girl. And I'm going to settle the score."

"Who took your girl?"

He glared at me. "John Cady. Her name was Alice Newman— and he slipped past me while I wasn't looking and took the last dance with her during the Annual Summer Wheat Harvest Picnic Dance."

"And then what happened?" I asked.

"Well that wasn't just the last dance of the picnic. It was the last dance ever," Sweets said. "He took her all the way to Roswell. And when we get there, he's going to get what's coming to him."

Larry "Sweets" Hovis played second base and batted leadoff for the Eskimos. He got the name Sweets, I learned, because he always put seven cubes of sugar in his morning coffee. He also wore the number seven on his jersey. Apparently, he also had carried this grudge for seven years.

"Sweets, I think you should let this go. It's time to move on with your life."

"After tomorrow, I will move on," he answered.

"What are you going to do?" I asked. He didn't reply.

~

Sweets disappeared sometime in the night and remained missing when we lined up for the national anthem the next day. He had also missed the brief practice we had conducted in the morning. When the Roswell chapter of the Volunteer Librarians of America finished their cowbell and triangle version of "The Star Spangled Banner," we could hear the engine of an airplane somewhere in the distance.

After the public address announcer called out the starters, I got a knot in my stomach. "Where is Sweets?" I wondered — because I knew he believed his nemesis to be in the ballpark.

The sound of the airplane engine moved closer. After a minute, we could see a bright yellow biplane descending towards the stadium. Clearing the outfield wall, it bore down on the seats behind home plate. Half the crowd held their breath, waiting for some stunt by the pilot. The other half scrambled for the aisles. An army helmet fell out of the cockpit as the plane reached the infield. Just a second later, Sweets slammed the plane into the press box occupied by John Cady. After patiently waiting for seven years, Sweets thought he had his revenge.

What Sweets didn't know was that Cady was already dead. Word around town was that Alice had decided her husband wasn't going to earn enough money as a PA announcer in Roswell to maintain the standard of living she desired. He was quite popular in town, but she didn't view New Mexico as the land of opportunity. The day before we arrived, Cady had been found dead in his bathtub, along with his microphone, which was plugged into a bathroom outlet. Foul play was suspected, and the police searched the town and surrounding area for the grieving widow who was the last known person to have seen him, but not a trace of Alice Newman was to be found.

The press box was empty for this game as a tribute to John's memory. A stand-in PA announcer was calling the game from the home team dugout. Understandably, the Rockets organization was upset. They were even more unnerved when they learned that one of our players was flying the plane. Sweets died on impact.

After many interviews with the police, calls to New York, and promises to the Roswell organization, I made my way back to the hotel. I crawled into bed and considered the events of the day. My second baseman was dead. We had no money, no home uniforms, and no hats.

"How could it possibly get worse," I said out loud. It was the wrong question. I should have asked, "How could it get any weirder?"

Nine

I woke up in the middle of the night. The image of the plane sticking out of the press box was all I could think about. Even worse, I had forgotten to call Thelma. As I fumbled for my glasses, I sensed somebody close by. I rolled over and there was Sweets. I yelled and fumbled for the lamp switch. The light failed to chase the ghost away. Sweets was in his uniform. Everything about him seemed normal except his eyes. They were completely black.

"I want to play for the Eskimos."

"Sweets, you're dead. You would have to bat eighth," I muttered. I started to roll over in hopes that the weird dream would go away.

"I'm not Sweets. However, I have taken his form."

"Then who are you?"

"I am Oiggamid. I have traveled to your planet as my people

do every summer. We take human forms and play baseball. My friends and I crashed last summer and I am alone and stranded. I wish to join your team. You welcome players that no one else will take. You have the black man and the Japanese pitcher."

"Korean," I corrected.

"I do not understand," Oiggamid said.

"Korean, not Japanese. Bobby is Korean."

"No matter. Please let me join your team."

"Those guys are Canadian. Besides, what makes you think I need you on my team?"

"The carbon life form known as 'Sweets' is dead. You have no second baseman. Without him, you lack speed at the leadoff position and you won't steal any bases."

"Well, you seem to have scouted us well. Since this is a dream and you won't be here tomorrow, yes, you can play for the Eskimos."

"Thank you. Should I wait on the bus?"

"That would be a great idea. I have a hard enough time getting my Canadians into hotels; I cannot imagine how tough it would be to ask the front desk for a room for my ghost, alien, whatever you are. Good night."

"Good night."

Sweets slipped quietly out of the room and I decided that if it was not a dream, the head injury must be the reason that Sweets thought he was from outer space.

The next morning, I walked out to the bus and slowly walked up the steps. Halfway down the aisle, a pair of legs stuck out from a seat. I crept down the aisle, hoping to find Turner or Ray. Instead, I found Sweets curled up in his uniform. He seemed shorter than I remembered.

"Sweets. Wake up."

His eyes opened immediately. They were still completely black.

"I am Oiggamid. Is it time to play?"

"No, the guys are just waking up and having breakfast. Sweets, do you remember the plane crash, going to the morgue, being pronounced dead by a doctor?"

"Yes, that is when I took the form of Sweets."

"Okay look, if that's the story you're going to go with, we'll have you looked at when we get to Portis. In the meantime, let's keep the outer space thing to ourselves, okay?"

"I'm fine with that, as long as I can play."

"Deal. However, we need to make up a story for why you are here before the rest of the guys get on the bus. Otherwise people will go crazy…"

I did not get to finish the sentence. Ray stepped on to the bus, took one look at Sweets, and sprinted down the street. He did not stop running until he reached the town limit. Then he sort of quick walked and looked over his shoulder every few steps.

Without alarming the rest of the team, I let Beanie know about our problem. "Beanie, there is one more thing I forgot to tell you about Sweets."

"What's that?"

"He thinks he's an alien."

"Aw, you're putting me on aren't you?"

"No, he really thinks he is an alien."

"Should we cut him?" asked Beanie.

"If he can still hit and play defense, I don't care if he thinks he's the Queen of England. However, we do have to keep him from scaring the other players."

I made up a story for the rest of the team about how Sweets had been knocked unconscious and the small-town Roswell doctor had misdiagnosed him. Then I told them he was acting strange and not to pay any attention to his alien ranting.

We found Ray a couple of miles out of town. It took most of the morning to convince him that Sweets was alive and he had not seen a ghost. He finally got on the bus; however, he kept a watchful eye on Sweets for the rest of the trip.

To calm Ray down, I asked Mort to tell us a little more about Portis. That's when I learned about the gypsies. On the north side of town, along the bend of Highway 281 and across from the Igloo, is a place called the Honky Tonk Café. The Honky Tonk was the kind of place of which Mrs. Shaw certainly would not approve. Next to the Honky Tonk, was an undeveloped area where gypsies often camped. Next to the gypsy camp was a gravel road and beyond that was Chick Lawson's Slaughterhouse. On any given night, one might find slaughterhouse workers drinking with gypsies and other unrespectable sorts. None of the Portis upstanding and fine citizens would dare darken the door of the Honky Tonk Café, save Mrs. Harrison once a year with a bucket of red paint tucked under one arm.

Technically, Osborne was a dry county. However, folks tended to look the other way since all the drinking was kept well north of town and the Church of the Brethren and the First Church of MethoBaptists formed a God-fearing buffer between the town and the booze.

They also tolerated it because it kept the gypsies happy. Unlike many other places, Portis actually welcomed their gypsies because this particular band seemed to have a knack for growing things.

Every spring, they would camp on the north side of town and wander the fields surrounding Portis dispensing advice to the local farmers. At first, the farmers distrusted the oddly dressed nomads. However, once they learned that the gypsies were harmless and their botanical knowledge was sound, the town grew to embrace them. Some residents, like Madam Kirkpatrick, even took to trading freshly baked pies for potions that kept her flowers bright and healthy all summer long.

"And that is why Billy Mudd's mutant dandelion won't die," said Mort. "The rumor is that the gypsies gave him some sort of plant elixir."

"Does this mean that ugly weed will be in right field forever?"

"I suppose so," answered Mort.

"That's great. I wonder if I could make a deal with the gypsies to kill it. Is this what my life has become? A year ago, I was in the Yankees clubhouse interviewing Joe DiMaggio. Now, I am asking gypsies to help me kill a weed. What happened to my life, Mort?"

Mort did not answer. I closed my eyes and listened to the chatter in the bus. Bits and pieces of conversation entertained me until I drifted off to sleep.

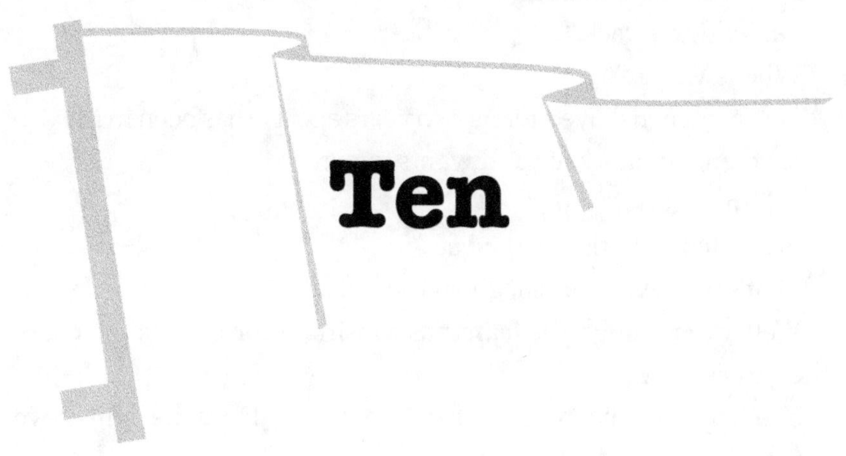

Ten

B am. Bam. Bam. "Valdez is back. Valdez is back," somebody shouted outside my door.

Bam. Bam. Bam. "Wake up Mr. Bennett, Valdez is back."

It was Wednesday morning. Two days before our opening game. Somebody was pounding on my door and yelling, "Valdez is back."

I could not see the front door from my bed, but I could see Lana. "Tell him to go away." Lana didn't reply. "You are going to have to start helping out around here or I'm going to let that crazy old lady evict you." She just stared at me silently.

"What?" I shouted as I opened the door in mid-knock. Mort knocked on my forehead. Then we just stared at each other. I blinked to get used to the light. Mort gulped and wondered if I was going to push him down the stairs.

"What do you want, Mort?"

"Sir, Valdez is back."

"Who is Valdez?"

"He's a pitcher. Played for us two years ago. He has been in Mexico since then, but he's back and wants to play."

"Is he any good?"

"Best pitcher Portis ever had sir."

"That's not saying much, given the last 20 years."

"Well, even though the team has a losing record, he won most of the games he started."

"You say he's been gone for two years. Does he still have his stuff?"

"Beanie's watching him throw right now. He told me to have you meet him and Champion at Frank's Café."

"Champion? Who is Champion?"

"That's Valdez' first name: Champion."

"Alright, give me twenty minutes and I'll meet you at Frank's."

I arrived at the café to find Beanie, Mort and Champion in a booth by the window. The same waitress that was working my first day in Portis was taking their orders. I had found out her name was Barbara. Every time I went to the café, she was working. At first, I thought she was just unfriendly. But the more I observed, I concluded she was just overworked and seemed preoccupied with something.

Beanie introduced our new pitcher. "Sir, this is Champion Valdez."

"Good morning," I said.

"Buenos dias, Señor."

"I understand you used to pitch for the Eskimos."

"Si. I pitched and called the games on the PA system."

"At the same time?"

"No, señor. I pitch every fifth day. But instead of sitting in the dugout on the other days, I sit in the booth and announce the game."

"Oh, I understand. Can I ask where you have been for the last two years?"

"In Mexico, caring for my mother. My father and grandfather were born in this country, but my mother is from Mexico City. When my father died, she wanted to move back to be with her sisters. She became ill and I took care of her until she died."

"I'm sorry you lost your mother."

"Gracias, señor."

"Who had the scrambled eggs," shouted Barbara. She startled us out of Champion's story.

"I did," said Mort.

Barbara proceeded to toss our plates down in order. I say toss because she indeed let go of each plate before it touched an outstretched hand or a table. So two of us had our plate crash in front of us, while the other two clumsily caught their plates midair.

"Is she always like this?" I asked.

"Yes," the others said in unison.

"I wonder why," I said.

"Rumor is that her husband left her on account of their kid," said Beanie.

"Yeah, they say the kid is retarded or something," added Mort. We all looked at him. "What? I've never seen the kid, so how would I know," Mort said. "I'm just telling Mr. Bennett what I heard."

I watched Barbara walk through the door of the kitchen. Her hand was outstretched towards the floor and a small arm and hand reached towards it, just as the door closed.

We ate our breakfast with Champion telling us stories about

playing baseball in the Caribbean league as a teenager. Apparently, he had gone to Mexico before finishing high school in Kansas.

"How did you get the name Champion?" I asked.

"My father won a bowling tournament the day I was born. It was the only thing he ever won in his life. He felt so good, he wanted me to feel that way for my whole life. So, he named me Champion."

I didn't say much the rest of breakfast. I mostly thought about parents. I thought about the fathers of Champion and Thelma. I thought about the mother waiting tables while her child waited in the kitchen. I thought about the pride of a champion and the legacy he left to his son. I thought of McClure, whose business and parental decisions were one and the same. And I thought of Turner, who would become a father by the end of the summer. Then I thought of the absurdity of running a baseball team to win a girl— and the prospect of never becoming a parent.

~

Even though we had done well in our warm-up games, I didn't get a whole lot of sleep the night before the season opener. Coyotes started howling at the moon just after midnight. That set off the greyhounds at Gubby Kaup's kennel on the south side of town. The dogs and the coyotes kept up their lively debate for several hours.

Between the lack of sleep and my uncertainty about our mission, I was a nervous wreck. I tried, somewhat successfully, to keep it from showing.

When I arrived at the ballpark, the 4-H kids were tending their own plots of grass in the outfield. The older kids dragged the infield and lined the base paths. Billy Mudd sat next to his weed in right field. From the dugout, it looked like he was talking to it.

Beanie tried to calm me down. He could see that I was nervous.

"We've got sixty of these, you know? Try to relax. Besides, if you're nervous, you will make the guys nervous. We're going to be fine."

"You think so?"

"Sure. It's a great day for a ball game."

Before the start of the game, we posed in the outfield for a team picture. The players were centered on a weed – Billy Mudd's weed to be exact. We wore road uniforms with Columbia blue and gold letters. On our heads were the Army helmets Mort had purchased. To give them added flair, Beanie had helped Mort paint a gold "P" on them. We looked ridiculous, which in retrospect, summed up the theme of the summer.

After the picture, the starters took their positions and Champion climbed into the tiny PA booth behind home plate.

Our opening day lineup included:

1B	Lester Davis
2B	Larry "Sweets" Hovis
SS	Joe Swift
3B	Henry Harrison
RF	Ray Robinson
CF	Travis Knox
LF	Turner (We still didn't know his first name.)
C	David Phelps
P	Bobby Park

The rest of us settled into the dugout. I studied the opposing team. The Vesper Turkey Vultures were mostly in their early twenties. They looked young and fast. But mostly, they looked mean. I suppose they were aptly named.

They say you can tell a lot about the upcoming season by the first at-bat. I have always partially believed this. However, the first batter of the 1948 K.R.A.P. League season left me puzzled as to our fate. On the very first pitch, the Vesper batter hit what appeared to be a home run. From the crack of the bat, everyone thought it was gone. The batter didn't even bother to watch it, choosing to run the bases and canvass the crowd for eligible ladies instead.

Also not watching the ball was a crow that had been, up until the first pitch, relaxing on the scoreboard. He chose that unfortunate moment to chase some food or go on some crow-related errand. He flew right in the path of the ball. The explosion of feathers froze the players and horrified the crowd. Meanwhile, the Vulture base runner, unaware of the demise of the crow and its subsequent altering of the ball's flight, continued his leisurely trot. He did notice that some of the girls were pointing to the outfield, but he assumed they were awestruck by his hitting prowess.

Suddenly, it occurred to Turner that the ball was still in play and he sprung into action. He grabbed the bloody ball and threw it towards home plate. Despite the aerodynamic challenge of blood and a couple of attached feathers, the throw was accurate. Our catcher tagged the Vulture runner and the umpire ruled him out.

This started a large argument from the Turkey Vultures manager, who lobbied for interference. I assumed the call would go his way until Mort, who had been mentored by Beanie very well, and knew the K.R.A.P. League Rulebook better than the people who wrote it, said, "The rulebook excludes crows."

"What? said the umpire. "Let me see that." He pulled the rulebook from Mort and read it aloud. "When a ball in flight comes in contact with an animal that has entered the field of play without permission, interference will be called and the play repeated."

"See, I told you so," said the Vesper manager.

"Read the asterisk," said Mort.

"The what?"

"Read the footnote at the bottom of the page," he instructed the umpire.

"I'll be damned," said the umpire. "Excludes crows. It says so right here."

"Give me that," said the Vesper manager who ripped the book out of the umpire's hands. He read it, threw the book in the air, and stomped off towards the dugout.

We went on to win the game by one run. And we won because a randy Vulture killed an oblivious crow. I surmised that success would come in unconventional ways. I was right.

Eleven

After winning on opening day, we lost four games in a row. However, our fortunes turned prior to a road trip to Geneva. Our hats arrived, just minutes before the bus pulled out. I took the Columbia blue hats out of the box and distributed them to the players and staff. I handed everyone a hat, but what they put on their heads was hope. The helmets represented nineteen years of futility. The hats meant an end to looking (and hopefully playing) ridiculous.

It worked. We won three games against the Gnomes and returned to Portis to face Fairbury. Awaiting us were our new home uniforms.

As I searched a box for my jersey, I asked, "Hey Mort, can I get another hat? I think I might have left mine in that hotel in Geneva."

"No problem, I have to get a new one for Sweets, too."

"Did he lose his?"

"No, I think that plane crash swelled his brain or something. He went up two whole sizes."

"You don't say." I thought long and hard about the conversation in my hotel room. Was I going crazy? Or was Sweets really an alien?

Mort flushed the urinal just as the Glenn Miller band finished a song on the RCA radio. The music made me forget momentarily that my office was a bathroom.

"I really like that song," said Beanie from inside the stall.

"Who is watching the store if we're all in here?"

Mort reached for the door. "Whoa, there," I said. "Stick those hands under the faucet before you head back out."

"Sorry, sir," he said and made his way to the sink.

"Beanie, do you have my sports page in there?"

"Yes, sir," replied the voice in the stall. "Do you want it back?"

"No, no. You keep it."

POST CARD

MESSAGE

ADDRESS

Dear Thelma,

Greetings from McPherson, Kansas! We won 2 out of 3 games on the strength of Ray's hitting. It took a little convincing that he was Canadian and not black, but they eventually bought it. Bobby pitched a complete game shut out. The Eskimos haven't had a shut out in 10 years, so folks will be excited when we get home.

Miss you much!   Love, George

Thelma McClure
798 Park Avenue West
New York,
          New York

~

Over the next few weeks, we spent most our games on the road. We continued to play well, considering the level of talent and our long history of failure. However, playing well wasn't good enough. We couldn't finish in the middle of the pack; we had to win the pennant. The town was excited that we were in fifth place. Beanie was trying to cheer me up on the bus, but the weariness of travel and the size of the mountain we had to climb wore me down. I fell asleep somewhere outside McPherson.

When I woke up, my head fell forward into the bus seat in front of me. Beanie, who had apparently been leaning on my shoulder, fell into the space between my seat and me. He sat up and we both looked around. We were somewhere.

Somewhere is the place you cannot define after falling asleep on a bus. There are no visual clues in the landscape yet to tell you if you are in Kansas or Nebraska. Endless fields of wheat stretch before your eyes, punctuated by the occasional clump of trees or a fence that is falling down.

It is human nature not to stay in Somewhere. Somewhere must be defined. It must be labeled. We must be in some county, some town, or some state. However, we must not just be Somewhere.

"Mort, where are we?"

"We are somewhere between McPherson and Salina. I would guess another hour before we get to Beaver City."

For everyone else in earshot, Mort defined where they were. I was still in Somewhere.

As the grogginess left me, I flipped through the league handbook to the Beaver City page. I noticed that the guide listed them as the Fur Traders and the Beavers.

"Why does the handbook have two names for Beaver City?"

Everyone at the front of the bus laughed. "Nobody told you about the Beaver City feud, huh?" said Mort.

"Feud? What does that have to do with the names?"

"It's the craziest thing you've ever seen," Beanie said.

"Forty years ago," Mort continued, "Cyrus Enders left the team to his sons. He had bought his way in to the league, but his doctor told him he was not going to live to see the first game. His two sons had been fighting over what to name the team. Cornelius wanted to name them the Beavers and Julius wanted to name them the Fur Traders. So, to settle the dispute, the old man put in his will that whichever nickname brought the most fans the first season would be the permanent name."

"So, that was forty years ago. What happened," I asked.

"Well, that first year, exactly 600 fans supporting the Beavers and 600 supporting the Fur Traders showed up to each game," Mort said.

"And?"

"And, for forty years, the two sides have filled every seat in that stadium. Nobody wants to give in," Mort went on.

"That sounds pretty crazy."

"Oh, you don't know the half of it," Beanie said.

"What else?"

Beanie continued, "Every top half of the inning the PA announces them as the Beavers and during the bottom half, they are the Fur Traders," Mort said. "In any given inning, they're being booed by half the crowd and cheered by the other half — and they're all hometown fans!"

"Well that's no big deal. That happens everywhere," I said.

"Not by their own fans… at the same time," said Mort.

"What about the visiting fans?"

The bus broke out in laughter. "No visiting fan has set foot in that stadium for forty years," said Beanie.

"You boys are pulling my leg."

"No, neither side can take a chance that a visitor might buy a ticket and then not go to the game. There are exactly 1200 seats and a Beaver or a Fur Trader occupies each one," Mort said.

"So what if one of our fans wants to go to the game?"

"They would have to sit on the grass behind the outfield. There is a hill looking down on the game where disinterested parties and visiting fans can take in the game," Beanie added.

"And you guys aren't putting me on," I asked.

Mort replied, "Just another day in K.R.A.P. League Baseball, sir."

Twelve

We won both games against Beaver City and were happy to be back in Portis for a week and a half. We gave the team a couple of days off practice to rest and mend any nagging injuries. Despite the days off from baseball, the store had to be open. Somebody had to sell tractor parts and fence materials and other farm-related products.

I really didn't enjoy that part of the summer. I liked meeting the people and I enjoyed the long discussions with Mort and Beanie about a wide variety of topics. I just didn't like selling tractor parts. It was painfully obvious to the farmers of Osborne County that I didn't know a thing about farming. Upon realizing this fact, they usually would ask, "Is there somebody else I could talk to?"

Even though I was supposed to be helping run the store, I mostly listened to Beanie and Mort make the sales while I did the clerical work. We agreed that this was the best system for everyone involved.

Before going to the store in the morning, it became a custom for me to eat breakfast at Frank's Café. On one particular morning, I was sitting close to the kitchen door. Each time the waitresses went in or out, the swinging doors revealed a brief glance at a little girl. I assumed the she was the same child I had caught a glimpse of weeks earlier. After watching for a while, I could see she was sitting on a little chair, quietly drawing pictures. An orange crate served as her desk. After a while, she saw me looking through the swinging doors and smiled.

"I'm Patty," she said in a voice that was hard to understand. She pushed through the swinging doors.

"I'm George."

She walked towards me and held up her drawing. "I drew this."

Her approach revealed the eyes of a child with Down syndrome. I could not say with any degree of certainty what Patty had created. However, she was proud of it, and was bound to show the entire diner. That is when her mom discovered she was out of the kitchen.

"Patty, what are you doing out here?" she cried, quickly trying to usher her back into the kitchen. I could tell that her mother was embarrassed. Was it the fact that her child had to wait in the café every morning? More likely, it was the fact that this child was different from all the rest. She didn't talk or look like the other children of Portis. Of course, Patty didn't know she was different and couldn't feel the eyes of the people in the restaurant. Her mother, Barbara, felt the eyes. She feared the eyes.

Barbara grabbed Patty's arm and made eye contact with me.

"She's beautiful."

"You don't have to patronize me," she shot back. "I know she is different."

I looked at Patty and back at her mom. "Does that make her any less beautiful?"

Barbara paused to consider all the mornings that she had hidden her daughter away in the kitchen. Now, her own fear of the eyes embarrassed her more than the little girl who was different from all the other children. I could see it in her eyes. She looked away from me and gazed at her daughter. She smiled and proudly took the picture.

"Let's put it in the front window."

"Okay, mommy."

Barbara escorted Patty through Frank's towards the front window. As they walked, Barbara looked back at me and smiled. After that day, folks noticed that the service at Frank's Café was a lot friendlier. They also noticed a little girl in the booth closest to the front door, proudly drawing pictures.

~

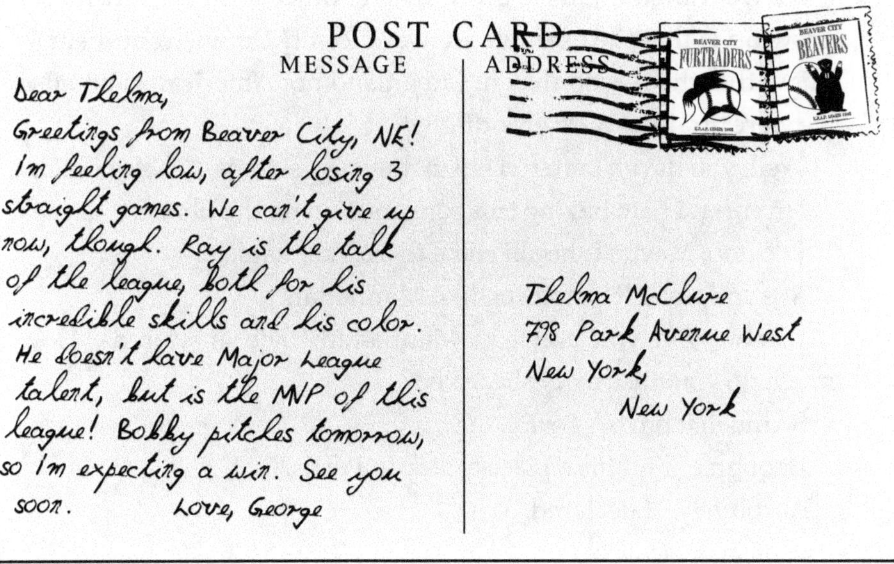

~

Later that evening, I called Thelma to give her an update. Mostly, I sent letters and telegraphs to her, but on this day, I wanted to hear her voice.

"How did you do this week?" she asked.

"We lost three out of four."

"George, this isn't working. How many games are you behind?"

"Seven, but there are still ten weeks left in the season."

"We are going to have to face the fact that you could fail. And if you do, I am not going to marry Rodney. We have to have another plan," Thelma said.

"What do you suggest?"

"How about Havana or Toronto?"

"Those seem like pretty extreme choices."

"Both are large cities that my father has little influence in."

"It feels like running away."

"It is."

"Do we want our kids to grow up in another country? When they grow up is that the example we want to set? Do we want them to know that the reason they're Cuban and not American is because we were afraid of their grandfather?"

"Well, you haven't offered any better suggestions," Thelma said.

"I'm sorry. I hate having this conversation on the phone."

"I do, too. Maybe I should come there," she said.

"Are you sure? It is nothing like Manhattan."

"I know. But you aren't in Manhattan," she answered. "How much do you miss me?" she asked.

"So much it hurts," I said.

"Enough to find me a place to stay in Portis?"

"Absolutely," I declared.

"Okay, I'll leave New York by train tomorrow," Thelma said. "I can call you from Kansas City and let you know when I expect to arrive in Portis."

"Okay. I'll book you a room at the hotel," I lied. There was no hotel in Portis.

"Is there running water at the hotel?" she said, sarcastically.

"Yes, but no indoor toilets."

"You had better be holding flowers."

What I didn't tell Thelma was that all three losses were against Red Cloud. I was really nervous before our first game against Red Cloud. I think I had the bus driver pull over at least three times so I could throw up. My whole future depended on beating this team.

I wondered if Rodney was aware of the challenge McClure had given me. Within a few minutes at Red Cloud's stadium, I knew. A tall man, well groomed and confident, walked directly up to me. Pausing inches only inches from my face and leaning in, he said, "You and this joke of a team are finished after this season. I don't care how many Canadian Negroes you bring in, they will never be as good as the Arrowheads."

Ray overheard and stepped in between us. "George, do you need me to show this guy some manners," Ray asked.

Ray's size intimidated Rodney, forcing him to step back a few steps. "I don't think you're really from Canada. I think Commissioner McGillicuddy should look into this," Rodney said. Turning to me, he said, "Thelma will come to her senses and she will marry me. You're a nobody. She will realize that one way or another."

That was just the motivation I needed. I was determined even more to win the pennant. Unfortunately, the rest of the team wasn't quite as motivated as I was, just yet. We lost both games of the double header. When I got to my room in the hotel, there was a note on my bed that said, "The best man won today, and will keep winning. Give up, Bennett."

The next day we lost again. I wasn't sure how we were going to turn things around, but when I got back to Portis, there were more pressing issues waiting for us.

~

Cornelius H. McGillicuddy was the league's Director of Rules Enforcement. Ironically, he was demoted from League Commissioner for his ill-fated change of the rules in 1939. That year, he had changed the rules of the game so the players ran to third base after hitting a ball instead of first. Players who walked or were hit by a pitch ran to first. This perversion of the rules had consequences when runners were on first and third because they were running in the opposite directions. Local newspapers began to include runner collision in their box scores.

The experiment lasted only one season and Cornelius was removed from office. Although he still had a job, he carried a wicked chip on his shoulder and was loathed throughout the league.

McGillicuddy began to hear rumors and complaints that the Portis team had employed colored folk, Japanese pitchers, and heaven only knows what else. So, Cornelius decided to get right out to Portis to investigate for himself.

The K.R.A.P. league office was located in Topeka, just across the street from the Topeka Daily. William Snyder was the sports editor and a friend of mine from college. He tipped me off about the plan.

Cornelius McGillicuddy stepped off the train with one suitcase in his hand and one purpose on his mind: exposing a scandal. If he could uncover malfeasance by a team on a wide scale, it just might help him regain the commissioner's job.

Inez Walker spotted him first and told Mrs. Shaw. She and Inez were often seen walking together in the early afternoon, trading recipes and gossip. Mrs. Shaw looked Cornelius up and down and decided that he was either a slick businessman or might be bringing whores to Portis. At any rate, she wanted no part of him and let him know it with a loud "harrumph" to accompany the nodding of her head and crossing of her arms.

Inez, however, valued information more than moral scorn and thus spoke to the well-dressed man.

"Sir, are you visiting someone in Portis?"

"Yes. I'm looking for the Eskimos' offices. I understand they are near here." He wiped sweat from his forehead with a bright red kerchief.

"You are a little old to be playing baseball."

"Ma'am, I may be in my sixties, but I have the vigor of a much younger man."

He winked, causing Mrs. Shaw to deliver another "harrumph."

"However, I'm not looking to play," he continued. "I'm looking to meet with a Mr. Bennett."

"I knew it," said Mrs. Shaw. "He's probably bringing whores to Portis."

Both Cornelius and Inez looked at Mrs. Shaw.

"Is Mr. Bennett engaged in illegal activities?" Cornelius asked. "Because I'm here to investigate league rules violations."

Inez found this turn of events to be quite delicious. She proceeded to tell Mr. McGillicuddy the whereabouts and heretofores of the Portis Eskimos. By the time she was finished with him, he was as zealous as a tent preacher in a town full of sinners.

Worked up by the tales of mischief from Mrs. Shaw and Inez, Cornelius burst into the store and demanded to see me. I could hear him shouting from where I was calculating the week's ticket sales inside the bathroom. Mort pointed to the bathroom door and said, "He's in there."

"I'll wait." He sat down upon his suitcase and opened the newspaper he had purchased along the way. After twenty minutes he looked up from his paper and asked Mort, "How long is he going to be in there?"

"Oh, 'til about closing time. He's got a lot of figurin' to do."

McGillicuddy looked at the door in amazement. "When is closing time?"

"Around five," Mort replied.

"You expect him to be in there for another four hours? I can't wait that long."

"Then go in there," Mort said.

"But it's not polite," McGillicuddy said.

"He won't mind," Mort said. "I'm sure he would welcome the interruption."

"You people are incredible. I have been to some backwater places before, but you take the cake."

"Thank you," Mort said.

"I meant that as an insult."

Beanie and Mort looked at each other and shrugged. McGillicuddy got up the courage and walked into the bathroom/office. "This is your office?"

I looked up from my desk and studied him. He was in his sixties and wore a black suit. (An unusual choice for July.) He held a red handkerchief and was constantly wiping his forehead.

"This is the best my employer had to offer," I began. "May I help you?"

"I hope so. I am Cornelius McGillicuddy from the K.R.A.P. League office. I am investigating some possible complaints about your team."

"What complaints?"

"Do you have a Negro on your team?"

"We have a Canadian, sir," I answered.

"But is he colored?"

"The rules state…"

McGillicuddy cut me off. "Don't quote me the rules! I enforce the rules. I am the rules!"

"Sir, with all due respect," I tried again, "the rules state that…"

He cut me off again. "There will be no colored players in my league," he barked.

"Your league? I don't think it is your league any more than I think that all the owners agree with this rule," I countered.

"You mind your tongue, Mr.," he said.

"Hey," I said, "aren't you the guy that tried to change the direction of the basepaths?"

His face was boiling red now. "You will regret this. I'm going to forfeit all your games and kick Portis out of the league." He stormed out, slamming the bathroom door behind him.

Beanie and Mort rushed into the bathroom after he left. Apparently, they had listened to the entire conversation.

"What are you going to do?"

"Maybe the gypsies can help," I answered.

~

I spent the rest of the afternoon at the Honkey Tonk Café, talking with the gypsies. I needed an angle –- some way to get McGillicuddy off our backs. So, I struck a deal with the leader of the gypsies, a man named Rafael.

"How can we be of service?"

"You said you were leaving town late tonight," I told Rafael. "I was wondering if you could take somebody with you?"

"You have a friend that wishes to travel with my people?" Rafael asked.

Music played as we talked, and a woman danced by herself near our table. "Well, he doesn't wish to per se — he's going to need some convincing," I said.

"You wish us to kidnap this friend?"

"I think kidnap is a little strong. My friend is a little tense and I think you," I pointed to the dancing woman, "and she could help loosen him up."

"Ah, she has the power to take the cares of the world away from any man," Rafael said. "But what price are you willing to pay for the liberation of your friend?"

"Fifty dollars," I responded.

"It is good that you wish your friend happiness. But I sense you wish him to seek that happiness far away from Portis." He leaned back in his chair, wiping sweat from his bald head. Then, leaning in closer, he said, "fifty dollars will only take him a few counties away."

"How far away and how happy will he be for a hundred dollars?"

Rubbing his goatee, Rafael replied, "It will certainly get him out of the state. His happiness may not be sufficient to keep him away."

"One hundred and fifty," I bargained. "That's all I can spare."

"Your friend is lucky to have you. He will travel by train to Colorado, I think. Along the way, he will encounter much happiness. He will forget his cares and never return to Kansas."

I had to borrow from Mort and Beanie and even Champion. But, I came up with the money and gave it to Rafael. The next morning, the town was buzzing about the guest who disappeared from Beaman's Bed and Breakfast during the night. Years later, on a business trip, I stopped in Colorado Springs. Near the outskirts of town I saw a sign that read, "McGillicuddy's Gypsy Campground, three miles."

Thirteen

I couldn't sleep the night before Thelma arrived. It could have been nerves or excitement or both, but I wasn't sleeping. So, I went to the store early and unpacked boxes that had come in the afternoon before. By the time Mort and Beanie got in, I had shelved the entire shipment. We then spent a couple of hours debating who was the best second baseman of all time until it was time for lunch.

Beanie and I arrived at the bus station at 12:45. He parked the Radio Flyer in front of the flowerbed on the side of the building. The wagon somewhat shielded me as I knelt down to pick a handful of daisies to give to Thelma. Then we leaned against the wall and listened for cars.

Inside we could hear the postmaster whistling as he sorted mail. His tune was the perfect accompaniment to the gossip melody

Inez Walker was performing. Was she singing or gossiping? For Inez, they were the same. "Singipping," I guess you could call it.

After a rousing chorus of "Clara Buehler is really a Bleached Blonde," (sung to the tune of "When the Saints Go Marching In"), I heard the engine. Gazing into the horizon, heat waves parted for the silver bus. It soon was in front of the station. At first, I could not see Thelma's face through the window. The sun reflecting off the bus blinded me. I had to blink a few times. However, in a moment I could see golden curls. Then an arm appeared, pressed against the window. The arm waved and a smile appeared. The sun blinded me from seeing the bus. Then Thelma blinded me from seeing the world.

When Miss Thelma McClure stepped off the one o'clock bus at the Portis bus station, time stopped. I never thought I would see her, or myself, in such a tiny town. But just like me, love led her to Portis. Residents were treated to their first glimpse of a Manhattan socialite. Her yellow dress with the floral print, pearl necklace and earrings, high heels and white hat with a yellow ribbon were collectively out of place.

Beanie stood up straight and adjusted a nonexistent tie. Champion Valdez, who was there buying stamps, whistled aloud. In addition, Inez Walker, whom no one could out-gossip, began writing copious notes in the margin of her newspaper.

I approached her with my flowers, but she brushed them aside, wrapped her arms around me and kissed me. It was a long kiss, and a good one. Good enough that Inez picked up the phone to sound the Portis gossip alarm. Long enough that Beanie began to clear his throat.

"Sir, the lady's bag?" said the bus driver.

I held out my arm for the bag and kept kissing.

Beanie said, "Why don't I just get that."

I heard Inez say, "Her tongue is practically down his throat."

I pulled away. "I missed you, too."

Thelma looked at the flowers, then looked at the nearby denuded flowerbed. "I see you're still shopping at the same florist."

"Can you believe they have a branch right here in Portis?"

She shook her head. "Fascinating."

Beanie cleared his throat again.

"Oh, I'm sorry," I said, recovering. "This is Glen Bush. Everyone calls him Beanie."

"Nice to meet you." She shook his hand.

"Nice to meet you, Miss Thelma."

We left the bus station and walked towards Frank's. I held Thelma's hand and her suitcase. Beanie followed with his wagon, but left us at the café. As soon as we entered, Patty greeted us at the door with a picture. Thelma kneeled down to thank Patty for the picture, while I glanced around the room. It was obvious that Inez had announced our arrival.

"Everybody is staring at me," Thelma said as she stood back up.

"Let them stare. You're beautiful," I said as we slid into a booth.

"It's these clothes. I've got to get them off."

"I don't think that will stop the staring," I said.

"I mean, I have to get more common clothes."

"Oh, I see. You mean to fit in."

"Exactly."

"Well, I think you look wonderful."

"That's very sweet, but I don't look Kansas," she said.

"Do I look Kansas?"

"You look very Kansas."

"Is that good?" I asked.

"I don't know. But I think it's growing on me."

"So, how long are you going to stay?"

"A couple of weeks."

"I wish you could stay the rest of the summer."

"I know, but Daddy will be mad enough about this."

Barbara came over to take our order. Patty followed with another picture and crawled into the booth, nearly sitting on Thelma's lap. Barbara and Thelma started talking as if they'd known each other their whole lives. It always amazed me when women — especially women with as different backgrounds as the two of them — did that. Patty and I got bored and started making faces at each other across the table. When they finally paused to take a breath, I jumped in and gave Barbara our order. She went back to the kitchen, but Patty stayed. Thelma's kind words and attention to Patty's picture captivated the little girl. She didn't leave Thelma's side until we left.

~

Thelma and I spent most breakfasts, lunches and evenings together for the next two weeks. She even accompanied the team on two short road trips. The players fell in love with her the moment she got on the bus to McPherson with homemade cookies. For a doubleheader in Vesper, she brought along brownies.

I never knew her to be skilled in the kitchen, so I was somewhat skeptical of the source of the baked goods. After much prodding, I learned that Inez Walker and Mrs. Shaw were secretly supplying baked goods to Thelma in return for discreet purchases of alcohol in the towns we visited.

It seems that both felt that it just wouldn't be proper for a lady to purchase a bottle of whiskey in Portis (even for medicinal purposes), so they needed a courier. For that service, they were willing to help Thelma endear herself to the players.

Of course, Thelma didn't need bribery to charm the guys. By the end of the two weeks, the team didn't want her leaving Portis any more than I did.

One particular morning, I had breakfast at the café by myself. Thelma said she had errands to run. What errands could she possibly have at 7:30 in the morning in Portis? When I finished eating I walked back to the Five and Dime to retrieve my notes from the previous game. Turning into the alley, I noticed the door to the apartment was open. I walked up the rickety metal stairs, hearing grunts coming from inside.

Before I could stick my head inside, an old woman let out a loud curse. It was a New York curse – definitely not a Portis curse. I entered to find Thelma and Mrs. Shaw, each with a crowbar. They were trying to pry Lana off the wall. Mrs. Shaw dropped her crowbar and rubbed her wrist and elbow. I'm assuming the curse came from her.

"Hello," I said.

Both women were startled by my return. "Umm. Hi, George," said Thelma.

"We're gettin' rid of the whore," shouted Mrs. Shaw.

"Yes, we're getting rid of the whore," Thelma added.

"I see that. You seem to be having trouble. Do you want help?"

"No, I think we're fine, don't you Mrs. Shaw?" asked Thelma. She obviously was embarrassed that I had discovered her errand.

"We were doing fine before you got here," answered Mrs. Shaw.

"It really sounded like you were making progress when I walked up the steps," I said.

"George Bennett, you can't possibly want to keep this lady's—"

"—Whore's," Mrs. Shaw interrupted.

Thelma glanced at her partner in crime. "*Whore's* picture on the wall. It's not decent."

"Well, I wouldn't want to be indecent," I said. "By the way, which one of you shouted that interesting word right before I walked in?"

Mrs. Shaw's eyes grew large and embarrassed. Thelma covered for her. "Why, we have absolutely no idea what you are talking about," Thelma said.

"Okay, I'll let you two get back to work. When you're done, maybe you could give this place a fresh coat of paint."

Thelma glared at me, so I left Mrs. Shaw and Thelma to deal with the whore, and returned to work. Sitting in my office, I was reading the Portis Independent. Amidst the local farm news, I found a story describing the world's reaction to Israel being formally recognized as a state. It had happened a few weeks back, but the news took time to get to Portis.

I was fascinated by the story, but was interrupted by a knock on the door.

"Come in."

Mort poked his head in the room. "Sir, the sheriff is here to speak with you."

"Oh, what about?"

The sheriff pushed his way past Mort. "I'll tell you what it's about. One of your players killed two of Paul Graham's cows last night. Did all kinds of unnatural things to them."

"How do you know it was one of our guys? We didn't get back from Vesper until after one o'clock in the morning," I responded.

"Well, one of your guys didn't go straight home. We found a ball cap in the pasture." He waved a Portis cap at me. "Who wears a size eight?"

Mort started to answer, "Doesn't Swee—"

I cut him off, "We lost all of our hats at the beginning of the year. Let me see that." I grabbed it from his hands and looked inside.

"Yes, sheriff, this is definitely one of the old ones," I said. "None of our guys have heads this big."

"What about that second baseman," the sheriff asked. "Curious looking fellow. He has a huge head."

"Who, Sweets? No, that's just a trick of the sunlight. If he played shortstop, his head would be as small as yours."

Mort nodded his head, but did not say a word. The sheriff looked at both of us with skepticism. He started to respond, but I said, "Now, go with Mort here and he will get you a couple of complimentary tickets to the game tonight."

He followed Mort out of the office, glancing back at me. I smiled, waved, and shut the door. I looked at Sweets' hat lying upside down on the desk. Why was Sweets killing cows?

Later that afternoon, I called Sweets in for a chat. Beanie sat in on the meeting. "Sweets, I need to ask you about these cows. The sheriff was here today. He thinks you might have had something to do with some of the local cows being mutilated. What do you have to say about it?"

At first he stared at me for a while with those strange black eyes. "Is it unlawful to hunt and eat meat?" he said, finally.

"No, but that meat belonged to someone else and it sure ought to be heated up a little before you eat it."

"Raw bovine is a delicacy on my planet," Sweets said.

"Sweets, enough with this alien thing. It's giving me the heebie jeebies. If you want to pretend to be from another world, that is your business. But while you are on this team, what you do is my business. No more cow killin' or you are off the team."

"Yes sir. I will comply for the duration of the season."

He turned and left the office as Mort entered, approaching the stall. "Did you just say 'killin'?"

"I believe he did," said Beanie. "I believe the city boy is getting more like us every day."

"Beanie, go get ready for practice. Mort, wash your hands." I wasn't happy about the implications of my altered dialect. I also was angry about Sweets. But mostly, I was mad that day that I was in Portis. On the other side of the world, Yankee fans were cheering as the team officially retired Babe Ruth's number. The Babe was being immortalized and I was not there to write about it.

Before I could get myself too worked up, Thelma burst into the office men's room and shouted, "George, I've got great news."

Mort zipped up quickly and tried to leave, but Thelma stepped in front of him. "Wash your hands," she ordered.

Mort looked to me for help. "You heard the lady, wash them." He sheepishly complied while Thelma finished her story.

"I found a place to stay for the summer."

"In Portis?"

"Of course, silly. It seems that a couple named Harrison are taking a cruise to Europe, to sort of rekindle their marriage. And they have asked me to stay in their house while they are gone."

"But you never have been a fan of the Midwest."

"It's starting to grow on me. And I'm going to work at Frank's Café."

"You're kidding. A prize-winning photographer for a major New York newspaper and you're going to throw it all away to be a waitress in Portis, Kansas?"

"It's just for the summer, and there weren't any openings at the Portis Independent. However, I'm starting to get the feeling that you don't want me here."

"No, it's not that. I just don't think you will be satisfied here. Besides," I said, "where are you going to shop?"

Thelma glared at me. "George Bennett, what a horrible thing to say. Do you think my life revolves around shopping?"

"I'm sorry. I really do want you to be here." I paused and looked around the office bathroom. "Well, maybe not right here, but I'm glad you are in Portis."

She studied me for a moment, deciding if I was sincere. "Okay, I'll accept that for now. See you at the game tonight."

She left the office and Mort entered with advice. "You probably should send her flowers for that shopping comment."

"Listening outside the door, were you?"

Mort turned red. "Yes, sir."

"So where do I get flowers in this town?"

"Lemon's Grocery has flowers."

"Alright, watch the store while I go buy some flowers."

Fourteen

During the summer wheat harvest, Portis doubled in size every day as farmers came to the elevator with their crops. It was unusually hot that summer and the constant emptying of grain into elevator and railcar left the town dry and dusty. That could easily describe how we played during that time. We lost seven in a row, surrendering all the ground we had made on Vesper and Red Cloud.

Down at the First Church of the MethoBaptists, the faithful were praying for the sky to open like a waterfall. I was just praying for a rainout. After the harvest ended, the farmers surrendered the town to the Gnomes. The Geneva Gnomes were a team we could beat. But I wasn't taking any chances. I joined the MethoBaptists on Sunday for some old-fashioned preachin' and prayin'.

It must have worked. The next afternoon, just before the first pitch, it started to rain. Everyone else ran for cover, huddled in the dugout or ducked inside their cars. Champion stayed in the announcer's booth. Within a minute, only one person remained on the field. I stood with my head tilted back, so every drop on my face could wash away the dust of the summer wheat harvest.

I could hear voices and I suppose they were telling me to come in out of the rain. I didn't care. The rain washed away the gritty dust. It rinsed from memory the disappointment of the seven-game losing streak. It submerged the disapproval of Thelma's father.

When it was done, Portis and I had been washed clean. I was standing in a little pond that took up most of the infield and forced us to cancel the game and reschedule the following day's contest as well. When the field dried out, we were ready to start fresh. I still love to feel the rain in summertime.

⁓

After the rainout, we played our best baseball of the summer. We won twelve of fifteen, pulling back into third place. The town was buzzing and I was trying innovative ways to keep them coming to the ballpark.

One particular Saturday afternoon, Mort said, "The bleachers look full tonight. What's the promotion?"

"It's 'Win a Cow Night,'" I proudly replied.

"Good thing he can't enter," Mort said while motioning towards Sweets.

"I did," Sweets said.

"You did?" Mort asked.

"You can't enter that contest," I said.

"I sure can. There is nothing in the rules that says I can't," Sweets said. "It only says you must be present to win. And since I'm on that lineup card, I am assuming I'll be present."

"But Sweets, the contest is for the fans," I pleaded.

"It does not say that anywhere in the rules."

"Don't let him bring that cow in here," said a frightened Ray. "George, if he starts ripping into that cow, I swear I will never play ball with a white man again."

"He hasn't won yet," I replied.

After the top of the third inning, the cow was led onto the field. She stopped briefly at the first base coach's box to relieve herself and then willingly settled behind home plate. Gladys Bush gracefully carried a microphone along with a burlap sack filled with contest entries. I closed my eyes and plunged my hand into the sack. Pulling out an entry I prayed, "Don't let it be Sweets."

It was. As 500 people anxiously awaited the name of the winner, I cleared my throat. "The winner is Larry Hovis."

A few quiet moments passed with fans looking around for a winner. Then, jeers and boos rained down upon the field as Sweets came to collect his prize. That's when things got interesting. Apparently, the cow, having seen firsthand what an alien second baseman could do to a cow, let out a moo, a shriek, or a "shrmook" and bolted for the outfield. Upon reaching the fence, it lowered its head and crashed through the wall without slowing down.

For reasons I cannot explain, the crowd took great delight in this turn of events and applauded. Sweets, however, did not take it so well. He pouted the rest of the game, committing two errors and failing to get a hit. I decided not to give away any more livestock during games.

~

Thelma bonded with Patty so well that she offered to watch her on days that Barbara was working. They spent most of the days at the city park on the Southside of town. They also could be seen frequently on Market Street skipping hand in hand. Patty loved to skip. And Thelma loved to hear Patty laugh. So, they often would skip from Clyde's gas station on the south side of town, all the way to the First State Bank where they would collapse giggling in the grass. It was an odd sight to some of the citizens of Portis, but they seemed to be enchanted by the carefree New York socialite and her curious little friend. I think for Thelma, it kept her mind off the impossible task before me and the implications of not succeeding.

One day I ran into the two of them at the post office. Patty was holding some letters while Thelma purchased stamps. "Good morning, ladies," I said.

Thelma seemed startled. "Oh, good morning. Why aren't you at the store?"

"Oh, we needed some stamps and I need to send this financial report to your father," I said. "Are you okay?"

"Sure, I'm fine." She looked nervously down at Patty.

"You seem worried."

She watched Patty walk towards the door. A dog was barking outside. Unable to resist the thought of a dog to play with, Patty dropped the letters and ran outside. Thelma chased after the little girl. When she re-entered the post office, I was holding the letters Patty dropped.

"These are from Rodney," I said.

"I was going to tell you, but I didn't want to add to your stress," Thelma said.

"Tell me what?"

"He and my father have been writing to me every couple of days. Trying to get me to leave. My father is pretty upset with me. He even threatened to have Rodney come and take me by force."

"You know I wouldn't let that happen."

"I know, and I really think he is bluffing. I'm sorry that I hid it from you, I just didn't want you to worry."

"I guess I understand."

"Do you want to read the letters?"

"No, I'll take your word for it. You know we're going on a three-day road trip. Maybe it would be safer if you came with us," I said.

"I don't think I can get time off from work. Besides, I'm a big girl. I can take care of myself."

The conversation paused while I paid for my stamps. "Okay, I'll see you later for dinner. We're leaving early tomorrow morning, so I won't see you for breakfast."

The next day, we drove to Geneva. After a doubleheader, we had two nights in Fairbury. While we were gone, I worried about Thelma. Rodney sent me threats as well. Just like Thelma, I didn't tell her because I didn't want her to worry. I should have taken his threats more seriously.

~

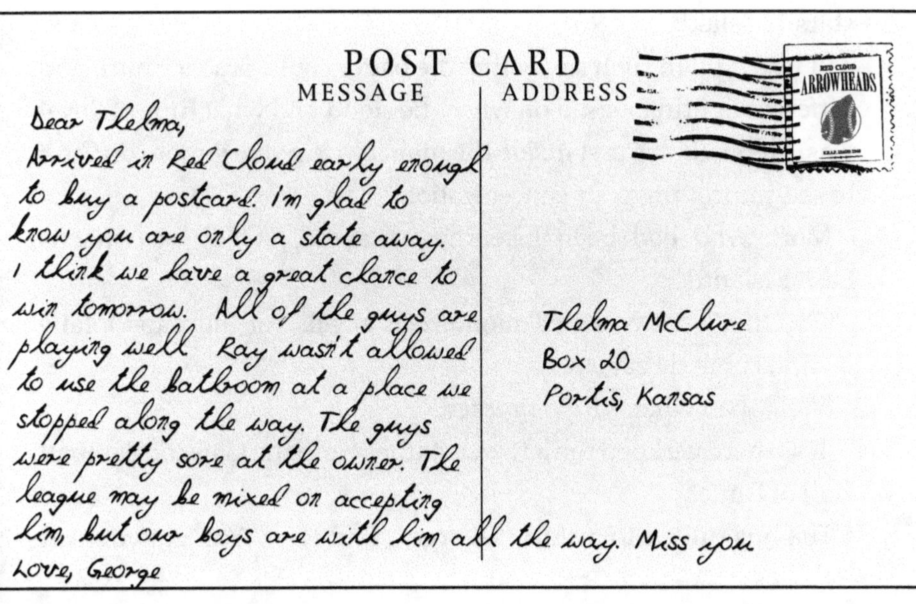

POST CARD

MESSAGE | ADDRESS

Dear Thelma,

Arrived in Red Cloud early enough to buy a postcard. I'm glad to know you are only a state away. I think we have a great chance to win tomorrow. All of the guys are playing well. Ray wasn't allowed to use the bathroom at a place we stopped along the way. The guys were pretty sore at the owner. The league may be mixed on accepting him, but our boys are with him all the way. Miss you

Love, George

Thelma McClure
Box 20
Portis, Kansas

~

During the trip, I sat next to Turner. He was a completely different person from the scared kid I met at the beginning of the season. Now, he was so proud of his yet-to-be born son, that he couldn't stop talking. Not being a morning person, I secretly hoped it would be a girl, just for keeping me awake all the way to Geneva.

He finally was interrupted by an argument between Sweets and Ray. I excused myself to see what the commotion was about. "What's the problem, gentlemen?"

"This crazy cracker still thinks he's from outer space."

Sweets replied, "I was explaining the structure you humans call Stonehenge. Ray doesn't believe me."

"Okay, just what is Stonehenge," I asked.

"It is a batting cage."

"You're putting us on," said Ray.

"No, I'm serious. It's a batting cage."

"If it's just a batting cage, why is it supposedly aligned with the stars," I asked.

"It was built in such a way that the batter could practice hitting in different lighting, based on where he stood and what time of day it was. The shadows cast inside the main circle make it more difficult to see, improving your concentration."

Mort, who had been listening in, asked, "Okay, so what is Easter Island?"

"Oh, that's not a sacred monument at all. You humans totally misinterpreted that one."

"Well, then what is it?" I pressed.

"It's where we keep the leftover statues from the Galactic Baseball Hall of Fame."

The bus pulled to a stop. "George," said Ray, "You got yourself one crazy second baseman." He and Mort scurried off the bus before Sweets could say something else. I looked at him and shook my head. "Batting cage? When we get back to Portis, I'm getting your head examined. Again."

The doctor in Roswell checked him out right after the accident, but said he would come to his senses in a few weeks. Between this and the cows, I was sure the crazy wasn't wearing off.

Fifteen

When we returned to Portis, Inez nearly jumped in front of the bus. She was frantically yelling for help. I was in the middle of the bus, so I couldn't hear what she was saying to the players who got off first. The players soon shouted for me to come quickly.

"That Rodney is over at Thelma's place. He's got her scared to death. She's locked herself in her room and he's drinkin' and carryin' on."

"Mort, I need your truck," I shouted.

Beanie, Mort, and I jumped in his truck and peeled out on Main Street. We charged south through town and turned onto Fifth Street. As we pulled up we saw Rodney push Thelma facedown in the backseat of his car and throw her suitcase on top of her. Before he shut the door, he locked it and ripped the inside handle off.

He raced to the other side of the car as she awkwardly fumbled for the lock. As Thelma tried to escape, Rodney pushed her back inside the car. He slammed the door just as I got out of the truck and started the car as I ran forward. His car engine revved and he peeled out just as I reached for his door handle. Thelma pounded on the window in terror, while all I could do was stand there in disbelief.

The smoke from his tires brought me out of it. Beanie and I raced to the truck and chased after them. The chase did not last long. The tired old truck that had served Mort for so long was no match for Rodney's Ford Super Deluxe. I felt my heart sink as his car faded away in the distance.

Beanie and I pulled to the side of the road after forty miles or so. The truck was overheating and we had not seen Rodney's car for at least an hour.

"What do you want to do? Follow them to Red Cloud?" Beanie asked.

"If I have to, yes. But, the truck isn't going to make it," I said. "Why don't we go back and I'll take the bus from Portis."

"You know, I think we're not far from Smith Center. Let's let 'er cool down, then drive there. I have a cousin there who owns a service station. Maybe we could borrow a car you could drive to Red Cloud."

After the truck cooled down, he headed for Smith Center Before we got there, we came upon a broken-down tractor in the road. Several cars and trucks lined the side of the road and police were directing traffic. An ambulance sat in the yard near a farmhouse. Below a majestic oak, a car was smashed and almost unrecognizable. Between the tree and the house, the body of a woman lay motionless.

Thelma's body had come to rest face down on a bed of bright

green grass. Her left arm was clearly broken and her left leg seemed to rest at a strange angle. Her head was covered in blood on the left side. The ambulance drivers gently turned her over. She was unconscious and bleeding from a gash at the hairline. The drivers quickly treated her wound and put her on a stretcher. I insisted on riding with them to the hospital, but I had to ride in front. As we pulled away, I caught a glimpse of the car. I had not really looked at it when we pulled up, but a man was pinned against the steering wheel and not moving. No one was trying to pull him out. Rodney was dead.

~

When Thelma woke up, I was holding her hand. She moaned and reached for her forehead with her right arm. Her left arm was in a cast. Her hand moved along the bandage that concealed a dozen stitches.

"Ooh, my head hurts. So does my arm." She paused while her mind considered the rest of her body. "Ooh, so does my hip."

She looked at me and smiled. "I'm glad you are here, George Bennett," she said as she squeezed my hand. "Now, tell me why I'm here."

"You don't remember the crash?"

"The last thing I remember is Rodney shoving me into the car."

"He was drunk. He lost control and hit a tree."

"Serves him right." She looked at the curtain dividing the room and asked, "He's not over there is he?"

"He's dead. He was already gone when folks showed up to help."

She closed her eyes and thought about the future without pressure from her father to marry a man she despised. She didn't look happy that a man had died, but she sure looked relieved. I let her drift off to sleep and slipped out of her room.

~

When I stepped out to the hall, Thelma's father had just reached the door. Hubert McClure grabbed me by the shirt and pushed me against the wall. "This never would have happened if you hadn't brought her to Kansas."

I shoved him right back. "You had Rodney kidnap her. This is your own damn fault. We wouldn't even be here if you had let us marry back in New York."

"My future son-in-law is dead and my daughter is a cripple and it's your fault."

"You know, the sad thing is I'm not sure which bothers you more— that Rodney is dead or your daughter might be a cripple." I was not about to give up on her recovering just yet.

That comment sent McClure over the edge, and he punched me in the face. I fell to the ground and he kicked me in the stomach. He hurled his folded newspaper at my head and stood over me. I looked at him slowly, bracing for another attack.

"Go ahead and marry her. Nobody will have her now anyway." He stumbled down the hall. The weight of his disappointment and rage disoriented him as he walked. At the far end of the hall, he collapsed on a bench and wept.

I got up, felt the bruise on my face, and walked down the corridor. I sat down on the bench next to McClure. He did not look up, just continued to weep, his head in his hands. I leaned back against the wall and stared at the ceiling. As badly injured as she was, Thelma was not as broken as her father was. Each passing minute seemed to age him. He sat up, cloaked in the weariness of a man at the end of his days.

He turned towards me and said nothing. I could feel his stare but kept looking at the ceiling.

"I just wanted what I thought was best for my daughter. I was wrong." His voice trembled. "Please forgive me."

I looked him in the eyes, but could not find words to reply. So, I put my hand on his shoulder and nodded.

"When the doctors say it is okay, you both can come back to New York," McClure said.

"But sir, there are still three weeks left in the season."

"It's okay. The contest is over. You can marry Thelma."

"Sir, it's not that. It's, well, complicated."

"Well, out with it, boy."

"I want to finish the season. I want to see Portis win the pennant." I stood and looked out the window. I had no idea if I was looking at the town. "I want to win for this team. For Portis."

"But Bennett, I don't even think I want to keep it going for another year."

"Just let me finish the season. Wait to decide what you want to do with the team then."

"All right."

"Thank you, sir."

He stared at me awhile and said, "I truly am sorry." Then he rose to his feet and walked slowly down the hall, disappearing into the elevator. I didn't see him again until later that afternoon. He entered her room and I left them to talk privately. She never shared what they said to each other that day but I suppose they made their peace with each other. He seemed to treat both of us with more respect after that, and a weight seemed to be lifted from his shoulders.

~

Mort and I were waiting at the bus stop. I had called my brother in Indiana to see if his wife could help with Thelma. Although lots of folks had helped in town, I felt she really needed Roxy's personality to cheer her up and speed her recovery.

We had not waited long before we heard the sound of an engine roaring. Then came the squealing of brakes. We ran outside in time to see two passengers emerge from the bus and vomit near a flowerbed. Inside could be heard several moans and one infectious laugh. Out sprang Roxy in a flower-print dress and a bus driver's hat.

"Hello, George," she shouted and threw her arms wide.

I hugged her and asked, "Did you drive the bus?"

"Sure did. All the way from Kansas City. The driver got sick and they were going to delay us a day. So, I tossed him in the back seat, borrowed his cap, and hit every stop between here and Kansas City."

"I can't believe it."

"And I got to every town ahead of schedule."

"Now, that I do believe."

I helped her with her bags and we walked to Thelma's house. Roxy seemed to brighten Thelma's mood, so I left them to get acquainted.

After Thelma had a few days at home to adjust, I called upon her one Thursday afternoon. We had just returned from a road trip, winning games in Moonlight and Minden. Roxy let me in the front door and ushered me into the living room. There sat Thelma in a bright blue dress, reading a magazine. For a moment I just took her in. A whimsical print turned her blue dress into a delicate suit of armor — temporarily shielding her from the horror of the past few weeks and the gravity of the days to come.

"George Bennett, don't just stand there and gawk. Haven't you ever seen a woman in a wheelchair before?"

"Not one as pretty as you." I kissed her cheek and kneeled down beside her chair. "Are you up for a little adventure?"

"Why, you sweet devil? What do you have in mind?"

"It's a surprise, but we have to get going now."

"Oh, I like surprises. Wheel me out of here."

I maneuvered the chair out of the living room and out of the house. Roxy was in on my plan, so she didn't ask where we were going. I pushed her toward the horizon, west of downtown. Thelma didn't question the plan until we passed the last house on State Street.

"George, where are you taking me?"

"Just a little farther," I said. "You see that barn?"

"Up on the right?"

"Yes, the surprise is behind that barn."

"You are not going to make me milk a cow, are you?"

"No, I promise this doesn't involve work or animals."

She leaned back and enjoyed the warm sun on her face. She may have even drifted off to sleep as I pushed her down the road. Asleep or not, her eyes were closed when we reached the other side of the barn. "Open your eyes, we're here."

Thelma opened her eyes and let out a gasp. "George, you remembered your promise."

In front of us stood a nearly inflated hot air balloon. It was yellow with blue trim and it cast a large shadow where we stood. I pushed her right up to the giant basket where two men were preparing to leave.

"We are almost ready, Mr. Bennett," one of them said. "Good evening, Ma'am."

With that, he hoisted a makeshift bench that would allow Thelma to sit and still see over the sides. Then we lifted her into the basket. After a few more preparations, we were untied and gently ascending into the Kansas sky. It wasn't a private moment, inasmuch as the pilot was with us. But it was the closest thing we'd had to romance since I had left New York.

"The world looks simpler from up here," said Thelma. "Less complex."

"I suppose you're right."

"I guess I might not feel the same if I was looking down from a Manhattan skyscraper. Maybe it's the green of the grass. Maybe it's the orderly acres of wheat and pasture. Maybe it's the company."

She squeezed my hand and continued. "When this adventure started, I couldn't imagine leaving all the conveniences of New York. But now, the one thing I crave most is the one thing Portis has in abundance: simplicity."

"Are you saying you would like to stay here?"

"Yes, I think we should stay here. I know that means giving up the paper when this is over, but we can't go back."

"What about your legs? You need the best doctors in New York if you are going to learn how to walk again."

"I can learn anything, anywhere. A five-year-old at the café taught me that. Besides, my father said he would pay to send a doctor here for a few weeks to help me."

"I can't give up being a writer. I like baseball well enough, but reporting is what I was born to do. Not selling tractor parts in your daddy's store. No offense."

"None taken. So, you don't want to stay?"

"I didn't say that," I answered. "I just don't want to work at the store. Maybe there is another way." My voice drifted off as I thought about my options. Thelma looked at me with curiosity, but didn't interrupt my scheming.

I held her close and we remained silent for the rest of the ride. After about a half hour, we descended to earth just as the sun escaped Kansas and hid somewhere behind Colorado.

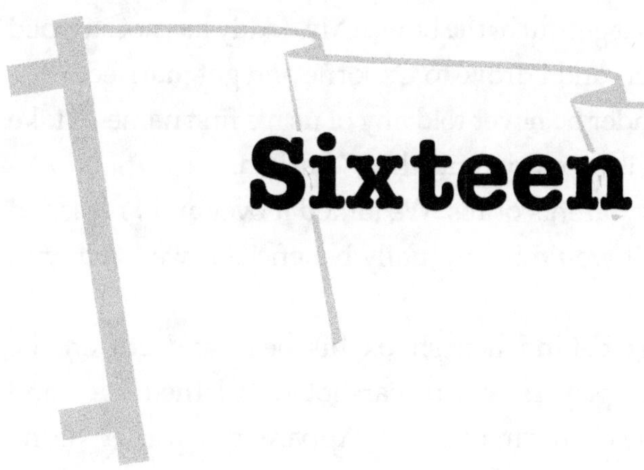

Sixteen

Thelma and Roxy continued to grow close, but after a few weeks, I could tell that Roxy was getting restless. Her loyalty and dedication never would allow her to complain, but I could see she was growing weary of being cooped up. So, when we had an away game scheduled in Red Cloud, I offered her the chance to ride along. We thought the bus ride would be too uncomfortable for Thelma, so Barbara and Patty spent the day with her.

Roxy met me at the store to catch the team bus. The players were climbing aboard, including the new Mrs. Turner. The week before, the Justice of the Peace in Osborne had married Turner and Sally. This was done over the objections of her father, who wanted a large Portis wedding for his only daughter.

"Why, Mrs. Turner, you look absolutely radiant today," I said.

"Will you be joining us on the road?"

"Yes, I simply must get out of the house. My daddy has not stopped crying since Francis and I drove to Osborne and got married."

Francis? No wonder he never told any of us his first name. "I take it you are living with your parents then," I asked.

"It was either my parents or his. We talked it over and I reasoned with Francis that it would be mutually beneficial if we lived with my parents."

Turner, standing behind her, shook his head and got on the bus, while several players within earshot rolled their eyes and whispered "Francis" in amazement. Apparently, Turner didn't find the living arrangement mutual or beneficial, inasmuch as he was still frightened of her father. Nevertheless, Sally took her seat next to her slumped over and sad-faced husband while Roxy positioned herself across the aisle. I had a feeling that Roxy was about to dispense years of marital wisdom upon that young couple all the way to Red Cloud.

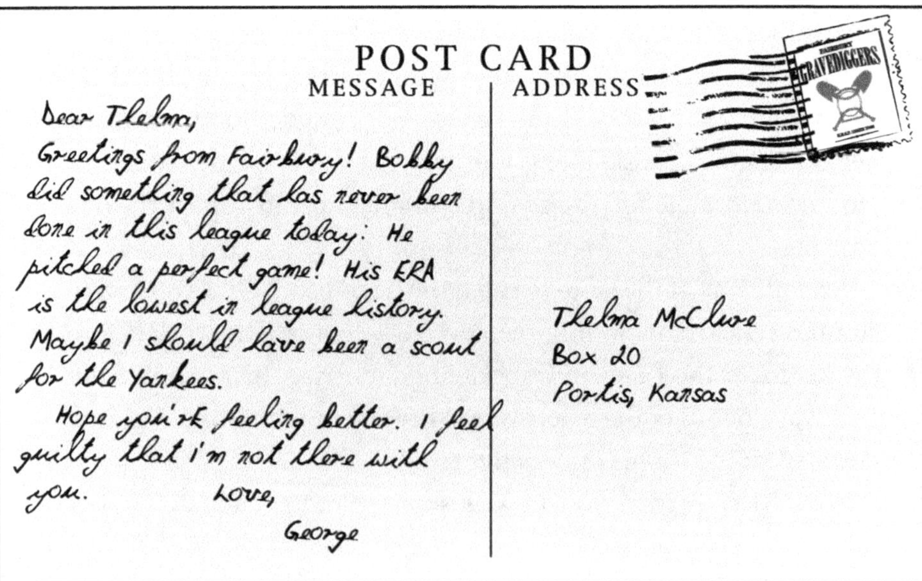

~

"Mr. Bennett, we got a problem," Bobby exclaimed.

Beanie and I looked at each other and rolled our eyes. We had defeated Red Cloud and were on our way back to Portis.

"What is it?" Beanie asked.

"Sally is having a baby," he answered.

"Now?" Beanie and I asked.

"Now," he answered.

Beanie and I ran to the back of the bus. Turner looked as pale as Sweets. He stuttered out the words, "How much longer do you think she has?"

"I don't know. I'm not a doctor," I said. "Somebody get Roxy."

Ray woke Roxy and brought her back to Sally. After a few questions, Roxy said, "I would say she has got about an hour. Let's turn around and go to the hospital in Red Cloud."

"There is no way I'm having my baby in Nebraska," Sally said. "Get me back to Portis."

"There is not enough time," Roxy said. "We have to take you to Red Cloud."

Sally grabbed the bar on the seat in front of her and bent it with her bare hand. She screamed, "Get me back to Portis!"

"How far is Portis, Beanie?" I said.

"'Bout one and a half, two hours, I guess."

I looked at Roxy and nodded towards the front of the bus.

"Time to change drivers?" she asked.

"Yeah, I think so," I said.

Roxy laughed as she stood and trotted up the aisle. I could hear an argument coming from the front so I went to investigate.

"Mr., if you don't pull over and let me drive I'll yank you out of that seat with my own hands," Roxy said.

"I would like to see you try," the driver replied.

She grabbed him by his neck and he started to swerve.

"Roxy, let go of him," I said.

I pulled Roxy off the driver and ordered him to pull over. "Mr. Bennett, if you let this woman drive this bus then I'm giving you my resignation."

I looked at Roxy and she shrugged her shoulders. Then she pulled the release for the door and kicked him out into the night. "Mr. Bennett accepts your resignation," she said. Then she climbed into the driver's seat, adjusted the mirror, threw it in gear and stepped on the gas. Roxy was racing to Portis.

Roxy made incredible time although most of the players were terrified at her speed, especially due to the rain. As we got closer to Portis, we heard a radio report about a bridge being out over the Solomon River. Because the radio was going in and out, we were not sure where. I knew we were getting close but I went to check on Sally. When I came back up the aisle, I felt us gaining speed.

"Roxy, did you know there is a bridge out?"

"Look out the side window."

I looked out to see the river below us. Then I looked straight ahead in time to see the other side of the bridge as we hit with a thud. Sally's water broke on impact, but now we were only minutes from the hospital. By now, every man on the bus was terrified of either the woman driving in the front or the woman screaming in the back. They huddled in the middle, sobbing in fear and holding each other.

We finally arrived in Portis and the baby arrived fifteen minutes later. Sally was so grateful that her little girl was born in Portis that she named her Roxy.

Mr. Riddle, Sally's father, warmed up to Turner after baby Roxy came along and even offered to repair our uniforms.

Seventeen

After winning a double-header against Beaver City and sweeping a three-game series with Fairbury, we had a one-game lead on Red Cloud. On the final Saturday of the season, we played a late afternoon game against McPherson while Red Cloud played an early game against Vesper. Everyone was hanging about the store, waiting for news of the result. Inez Walker was there as well, given that this was the biggest scuttlebutt in Portis in the last twenty years. She was determined to know before the Portis Independent.

I snuck away for a lunch meeting with Mr. Kissel, owner of the paper. Nobody knew I was gone until I returned.

"Where have you been?"asked Mort.

The phone in the bathroom rang before I could answer. The entire team followed me into the bathroom office and stared at me as I answered the phone.

"Hello," I said.

The players looked at each other and whispered.

"They did?"

They could tell from my voice what happened.

"Okay, we'll call you when it's over."

I hung up the phone and shook my head. "Red Cloud won today." Inez Walker, whom I hadn't noticed before, left the men's room. "Was that…" I paused. "Oh, never mind."

"Hey, what is all the fuss?" asked Mort. "All we have to do is beat McPherson today and we win the pennant."

"They are throwing Lutz. We haven't hit him all year."

"Well, then our manager is going to have to think of a way to beat him."

All the players turned their eyes towards Beanie. "I'll think of something by the time we reach the field. Don't you boys worry. Ol' Beanie won't let you down."

The team filed out of the bathroom to walk to the game. Just before I walked out, I heard a voice from the stall say, "A little help?"

I grabbed a roll of toilet paper, tossed it over my shoulder and walked out. I heard a faint "thank you," just as the door closed.

Outside the store, the team lined up behind Beanie. He and Mort led the procession, pulling their wagons. The team walked single file through the town, along Mr. Riddle's shortcut and up the hill to the field. The Eskimos were making the last trip of the summer to the Igloo.

～

Thelma felt well enough to attend the final home game. We built a platform so her wheelchair could sit in the aisle next to Roxy.

Just before the National Anthem, Ray came over to me and took off his hat. I could tell there was something he wasn't sure how to tell me.

"Coach, the guys and I have been talking and we want to do something for Miss Thelma."

"Oh, what did you have in mind?"

"Something to show her, you know, how much she means to us."

"And?"

"Well, when we take the field today, don't worry about how we do it. We still aim to play hard." He walked out on to the field to join the others.

I looked at Beanie to see if he knew what was going on and he just shrugged his shoulders. "What's up, Bean?"

He threw up his hands. "Beats me."

When it came time to take the field, the starters left the dugout and stood side by side. Then they skipped to their positions.

"Why are they skipping?" Thelma asked with a chuckle.

"Because they love you," said Roxy.

The McPherson fans laughed at the skipping ballplayers. However, the Portis fans understood. The ones who usually stand up and clap stood a little longer and clapped a little louder. Meanwhile the lone Portis fan still in her seat wiped tears from her eyes, smiled, and said, "Play ball."

The bleachers were full by game time. Everyone in Portis and everyone who knew someone in Portis came out for the game. Bobby retired the side in the top of the first inning. We still did not know what Beanie's strategy would be. When Sweets came up to bat, Beanie gave him the signal to bunt. He made contact on the first pitch, but popped it up to the catcher.

Beanie signaled the next batter to bunt. After a few pitches, he bunted down third base line. With his speed, he was able to get to

first. Then the most curious thing happened. Beanie told Turner
to bunt. He looked confused by the signal and called time. I met
them both at home plate.

"Beanie, did you tell him to bunt?" I asked.

"I sure did."

"Why? You have a runner on first and only one out. Are you sure
you don't want to hit and run?"

"No, I want him to bunt. Trust me," Beanie said. He turned and
went back to the dugout.

I looked at Turner. "You heard the man, bunt!"

He worked the count full and I expected Beanie to give the swing
away sign. Instead, he signaled for a bunt. Turner stepped out of
the box twice to see if Beanie was sure. Finally he got back in and
made contact. The pitcher fielded the ball and they made the play
at first. Now there were two outs. When Ray stepped into the box, I
called time and Beanie came out.

"Beanie, there are two outs and Ray is up," I said. "Why are you
giving him the bunt sign? Is this your strategy -- beat them by
hitting the ball six feet at a time?

"Yes."

"Yes?"

"Yes," Beanie said. "Look, Lutz is the only pitcher they have who
is worth a nickel. If you get in his head and knock him out of the
game, we will pound their other pitchers. If he pitches a complete
game, we are going to lose the pennant. You know it. Our hitters
know it. And McPherson knows it. Haven't you noticed that he has
thrown more balls with each at-bat?"

"All right, you have not let me down yet. Ray, bunt."

When Lutz saw Ray square around to bunt on the first pitch
during his windup, he came unglued. He hitched his motion and
then held on to the throw, prompting the umpire to call a balk.

Sweets was now on third. Lutz composed himself and started his delivery. Ray squared to bunt again and he threw the ball over the backstop. Sweets trotted home and we had a one-run lead. Now the Marauder manager complained to the umpires while Lutz yelled at our dugout.

Then on the next pitch, Ray squared again. This time Lutz hit him with the pitch and Ray went to first. Lutz threw his glove and walked off the mound towards me, incorrectly assuming that I was calling for the bunts. "You tell one more guy to bunt and I'm going to knock your block off."

Of course, we told Lester to bunt, and it was on. Lutz tore off the mound and got in a few good punches before the team came to my rescue. It took ten minutes to stop the fracas. When it was done, Lutz was ejected but so was Lester. Over the next few innings, the runs piled up for both teams. Bobby just didn't have his best stuff and the bullpen wasn't helping. When the top of the ninth came, we were clinging to a one-run lead.

The first Marauder struck out, and the second got an infield single. The third batter hit the ball to Henry at third, but he only had time to throw to second. With two outs and the tying run on first, the Marauders' best hitter stepped to the plate. The runner on first was fast, faster than Sweets. A hit would get him in scoring position, but a hit in the gap would tie the game.

After a couple of teaser pitches out of the strike zone, Bobby delivered one down the middle. The Marauder hit a line drive near the right field line, forcing Ray to sprint to the ball. I was sure the game would be tied. However, something strange happened on the ball's second bounce. It stopped. Just as it should have darted past Ray, because it clearly was out of his reach, it stopped. He grabbed the ball and threw a dart to the catcher, who was blocking home plate. Phelps made the tag and the game was over.

Portis had won the pennant. The players piled on the mound to celebrate. After a few minutes, I finally got to Ray.

"Why did the ball stop? That thing should have gone to the fence," I shouted.

"It was that dirty kid's crazy weed!"

"What?"

"That mutant dandelion, the one Mr. Beanie would not let you pull. It caught the ball."

"Come on, are you serious?"

"I am telling you, that ball was stuck in that crazy weed. It looked like I was pulling it out of a green ball glove."

"Well isn't that the craziest thing you have ever seen?"

"Not in this league."

I looked at Sweets and Beanie, then to the Radio Flyers parked by the dugout, and finally to Thelma.

"Yeah, I guess you're right," I said.

Ray stuck out his hand and I shook it. "Thank you, George. Thank you for letting me play one more season."

"It was my pleasure. Thanks for hitting us into a pennant."

"You know if you were to decide to stick around, some of my Canadian brothers would like to play in Portis next year," Ray said.

"Really? You related to any second basemen, in case Sweets decides to go back to his home planet?"

"Boss, do you think he's really an alien or just crazy?"

"What do you think?" I said.

Ray stared at him for a moment. "All I know is, he sure ain't from around here."

"Neither are we," I answered.

Ray looked back at me and smiled. Then he looked at the bleachers. "I think Miss Thelma wants to congratulate you."

I changed clothes after the game and washed up. Then I met Roxy and Thelma for a stroll and some dinner. Along the way, we witnessed something glorious and terrifying. As we headed west, suddenly we saw a great flash of light on the horizon. After my eyes recovered from the brightness, I saw what appeared to be a flying saucer above Chester Lemon's wheat field on the west side of town. It hovered for a few moments, then rose and disappeared.

"Thelma, did you see that?"

"You don't think they came back for him, do you," she said.

"Who?"

"Sweets!"

"Oh, Thelma, you don't believe that story?"

"I believe what I just saw. What *we* just saw."

Thelma was right. Or, should I say, I assume she was right because Sweets never was heard from or seen on this planet again. I tucked the story away in my memory until 20 years later when I heard that one of the statues on Easter Island was missing. Did Sweets go into the Galactic Hall of Fame?

We spent the rest of the evening discussing all the strange and wonderful things we had witnessed during our summer in Portis. The three of us talked well into the night, knowing that Roxy would have to leave the next day.

We met for lunch the next day and spent the rest of the day together. The late afternoon bus arrived and we helped Roxy load her luggage. On the curb next to us sat the empty suitcase loaned to me just five months earlier. The only difference was the large yellow and blue "P" that Mort had painted on all of our suitcases. I mistakenly thought Roxy might need an extra case and had brought it along with me.

When the bags were in the bus, she leaned down and kissed Thelma on the cheek. "You take care of yourself."

"Thank you so much for coming to stay," Thelma said.

"It was my pleasure. I'll be back in two months for the wedding," Roxy added. Thelma and I had decided to get married in Portis, provided the First Church of the MethoBaptists wasn't booked.

I hugged Roxy and thanked her again. As she got on the bus, I heard her ask the driver, "You need some relief? You look kind of tired."

I laughed and looked at Mort and Beanie. Both were holding the handles to their wagons, loaded with equipment.

"The season is over. Why are you still pulling those around," I asked.

They looked at each other and shrugged. Then Mort offered, "Because you never know when you might run into a prospect."

"Yeah, you might need to test his arm or watch him hit," Beanie added. "A fellow never knows when he might need this stuff."

"So, what brings you two down here anyway? Did you come to see Roxy off?"

"No," said Mort. "We came to congratulate you on your new job."

I glared at Beanie, who immediately realized I might not have told Thelma the news, yet.

"What new job?" she asked.

"Sorry, I was going to surprise you tonight. Mr. Kissel is retiring from the newspaper business. I'm going to run the Independent next year."

"George, that's wonderful!"

"I thought you might be pleased. Of course, I'm going to need a good photographer."

"I accept."

"What makes you think I meant you? Mort's pretty good with a camera."

She glared at Mort who shrank behind Beanie. "Okay, you've got the job. Just don't hurt Mort."

I shook my head and started to push Thelma's wheelchair towards downtown. Beanie and Mort followed. We stopped and turned around when we heard the squealing of the bus tires. The doors flew open and the driver tumbled out onto the ground. A woman in a flower print dress stepped out, grabbed his hat and returned to the bus. A faint but infectious laugh preceded the sound of squealing tires and Roxy disappeared from Portis.

As we watched her drive out of sight, Thelma asked, "Do you think the driver in Kansas City really got sick?"

I laughed, "Not anymore."

I pushed Thelma towards the light of Frank's Café while Beanie and Mort pulled their Radio Flyers home.

"George, did you think we would wind up in Portis?"

"No, I suppose not."

"This peculiar little place was the farthest place from my mind five months ago. Now, it feels like home."

I stopped pushing Thelma for a moment and asked her to wait. I walked down the road a little and placed the empty suitcase by the side of the road for the next weary traveler who came to Portis. I didn't need it anymore, I was home.

∾ THE END ∽

Appendix I

K.R.A.P. League Final Standings 1948

(Courtesy of the K.R.A.P. League Historical Society)

Team	Wins	Losses
1. Portis Eskimos	39	21
2. Red Cloud	38	22
3. Vesper	35	25
4. McPherson	33	27
5. Fairbury	31	29
6. Beaver City	30	30
7. Minden	28	32
8. Geneva	24	36
9. Moonlight	23	37
10.Parallel	19	41

Appendix II

K.R.A.P. League Results by Year
(Courtesy of the K.R.A.P. League Historical Society)

Year	Champion	Runner-up
1903	Concordia	Geneva
1904	Concordia	Red Cloud
1905	Dorchester	Concordia
1906	Blue Rapids	Miltonvale
1907	Crete	Minden
1908	Blue Rapids	Crete
1909	Crete	Minden
1910	Crete	Geneva
1911	Crete	Geneva
1912	Geneva	Blue Rapids

K.R.A.P. League Results by Year - Continued

Year	Champion	Runner-up
1913	Miltonvale	Blue Rapids
1914	Moonlight	Minden
1915	Concordia	McPherson
1916	Beaver City	Portis
1917	Beaver City	Blue Rapids
1918	Beaver City*	Beaver City*
1919	Blue Rapids	Portis
1920	Fairbury	Vesper
1921	Beaver City	Portis
1922	Portis	Fairbury
1923	Blue Rapids	Vesper
1924	Moonlight	Blue Rapids
1925	Portis	Minden
1926	Beaver City	Portis
1927	Fairbury	Red Cloud
1928	Portis	Minden
1929	Red Cloud	Beaver City
1930	Red Cloud	McPherson
1931	Fairbury	Vesper
1932	Beaver City	Moonlight
1933	Minden	Fairbury
1934	Moonlight	Vesper
1935	Red Cloud	Beaver City
1936	Parallel	Red Cloud
1937	Parallel	Red Cloud
1938	McPherson	Moonlight
1939	Vesper	Minden
1940	Geneva	Beaver City
1941	Geneva	Fairbury
1942	Red Cloud	Vesper

K.R.A.P. League Results by Year - Continued

Year	Champion	Runner-up
1943	Beaver City	Vesper
1944	Moonlight	Red Cloud
1945	Vesper	Red Cloud
1946	Red Cloud	Moonlight
1947	Red Cloud	Vesper
1948	Portis	Red Cloud
1949	Portis	McPherson
1950	Portis	Vesper

Appendix III

K.R.A.P. League History By Decade

(Courtesy of the K.R.A.P. League Historical Society)

The fledgling K.R.A.P. league began in 1903 with six teams. The "Original Six" as they called themselves, were Concordia, Dorchester, Blue Rapids, Geneva, Crete, and Red Cloud. Concordia was set to play host to the first K.R.A.P. League game on May 5, 1903. The game was rained out. In fact, the first week of K.R.A.P. League games were rained out. Therefore, on May 12, 1903, Blue Rapids hosted the first K.R.A.P. League game. Not being able to claim host to the first game would cause much bitterness in Concordia. So much bitterness, in fact, that it would cause them to leave the league shortly after its inception.

Despite the bitterness, or maybe because of it, Concordia won the first two pennants, then left the league to join the Federation of Agriculture, Retailers and Tradesmen League. That league ran out of gas three seasons later and folded. Concordia rejoined the K.R.A.P. League the following season.

Dorchester won its only championship in 1905. The team disbanded the following spring after an inter-squad game led to a massive bench-clearing brawl. Without enough players healthy enough to play on opening day, the team decided to forfeit the season. Since there was one less team to play, many of the K.R.A.P. League teams supplemented their season by barnstorming throughout the Midwest and Maine.

Blue Rapids won its first pennant in 1906. The Blue Rapids Crawfish would be a dominant team in the league until 1925 when they left the league for spite.

Crete, Nebraska, won championships in 1907, 1909, 1910, and 1911. Their league dominance ended abruptly due to a brawl known as the Great Cretan Uprising of 1912. Cretan took up arms against Cretan in a civil war that lasted 49 minutes, cost three lives (a mule and two pigs) and left the ballpark in ruins. Unconfirmed reports lay the blame for the violence at the feet of a seamstress who wanted to change the team's colors to pink and black. A monument to those who fell that day was stolen in 1970 by University of Nebraska fraternity pledges. It never was recovered. Local residents claim the ghost of the mule still can be seen behind the convenience store that occupies the site of the old ballpark.

The absence of Cretans allowed the Gnomes to take the pennant. Geneva had finished second twice before winning the 1912 pennant. Some league historians believe that Gnomes posed as Cretans in order to start the Cretan Uprising. The Gnome-Cretan Debate, as this theory came to be called, was robustly debated in the liberal arts schools of Nebraska until the state legislature ordered a full investigation. The Nebraska Legislature report, called the Warren Commission after the name of the mule, concluded that a Gnome acted alone in starting the uprising. The Warren Commission report officially was renamed to Committee of Cretans report, due to the investigation into the death of President John F. Kennedy. This was done at the request of Nebraska schoolteachers who feared confusion in history classes. Within a few years, the debate faded from memory and Nebraska schoolchildren had to find other things to be confused about.

At any rate, the owner of the mule was convinced that the Gnomes were up to shenanigans and put a curse on Geneva's baseball team. The Gnomes would not win another pennant until 1940. Coincidently, the owner of the mule died just before spring training that year.

Miltonvale won the next year and promptly moved to McPherson. I don't mean just the team; the whole town moved. Miltonvale later was repopulated but failed to take to baseball the way the previous residents now living in McPherson did. However, they did field a Beer League Croquet team that won a national championship.

Moonlight won its first championship the following year. In 1915, Concordia won a third title and promptly left the league (again) for greener pastures. They tried unsuccessfully to rejoin the K.R.A.P. League each of the next twenty years.

Beaver City won the next three championships. Due to a tie in 1918, Beaver City and Blue Rapids had to settle the pennant with a one-game championship. This proved to be a difficult event as the game was played in Beaver City.

The Beaver City franchise had been the subject of a long running feud between two factions that couldn't agree on the official team nickname. One side called the team the Fur Traders and the other referred to them as the Beavers. The dispute could only be settled if the fans of one name outnumbered the fans of the other. With an abundance of spite only the Hatfield's and McCoy's could appreciate, the town had sold out every game leaving no seats for the opposing team's fans. Blue Rapids supporters could only watch from the outfield. After losing, they filed a grievance with league headquarters, but their protest went unanswered.

The following season was even more bizarre, inasmuch as Beaver City finished so far out in front, they insisted that either the Beavers and/or the Fur Traders be named second place. A shipment of plows had sunk in the Mississippi River that summer, leaving many farmers without new equipment. Beaver City had received its equipment early, leaving the town with a temporary corner on the market, and thus more influence on league decisions. The decision of who would be first was left to a coin flip. The Beavers' representative guessed wrong. He succumbed to a mysterious blunt force wound to the head the next night. His murder never was solved, but a plaque in his honor still marks the outfield entrance into the Fur Traders side of the Beaver City Stadium. Due to this very bizarre set of circumstances, the official K.R.A.P. record book shows Beaver City in both first and second for the 1918 season.

In 1919, the Portis Eskimos joined the league with immediate success. They finished a close second to Blue Rapids. The Eskimos would find much K.R.A.P. success in the Twenties.

1920 – 1929

The Twenties were good to the Portis Eskimos. They won three championships (1922, 1925, and 1928) and finished second twice. The decade also saw the exit of Blue Rapids from the league and the addition of Parallel and Fairbury, the latter winning the pennant in its first year (1920). Red Cloud began to emerge towards the end of the decade, beginning a league dominance that would last until 1948.

The 1923 season marked the final championship for Blue Rapids.

Moonlight won the championship in 1924, continuing what would become an odd pattern for its success: All of its championships came in a year that ended in '4' (1914, 1924, 1934, and 1944). No scientific explanation for this phenomenon has ever been found.

Portis took its second championship in 1925. The Eskimos' strength that season was pitching, with a pair of twenty-game winners on the staff. One of the standouts was Richie Bonisa, an ambidextrous pitcher who was a starter with his right arm and a reliever with his left. His record of ten saves of his own games is still a league record.

In 1926, Beaver City won yet another championship. The league had a down year for attendance and league officials came close to folding the league. (Except Beaver City, which continued to sell out every game.) At a meeting in Kansas City, it was determined that the league would continue for one more season.

Fairbury brought home the championship in 1927 and brought fans back to the ballpark, thus saving the league. The Gravediggers featured a midget and a giant pair that was popular in every city they visited. George McKeeman stood 7 feet, 2 inches and his catcher Eddy Sprout was 3 feet, 5 inches. This made for some comical conferences at the mound and accounted for Fairbury leading the league in passed balls. The circus, so to speak, took the focus off the amazing accomplishment of the pitching staff. They managed to post a 1.43 team ERA, a record which stands to this day.

In 1928, the Portis Eskimos claimed their third championship of the decade. The league's first night game was played that season.

Although Vesper had no lights, a wildfire burning near the outfield allowed the team to make up a rainout with Minden from the day before. The game was called after seven innings due to right field being consumed by flames. However, league rules require only five innings to consider a game official. Thus, the game is listed as the first night game in league history.

Red Cloud closed out the decade with the 1929 pennant. It was a tight race with Beaver City until the last week of the season. Several Beaver/Fur Traders were felled with a curious case of food poisoning after eating in a Red Cloud diner. Beaver City accused Red Cloud of tampering with their food in order to the win the pennant, but the accusations never were proved.

1930 – 1939

The Thirties began as the Twenties ended, with Red Cloud winning the championship. Red Cloud would finish in the top three for the next eighteen years, while Portis continued work on a nineteen year losing streak.

The Great Depression cut many of the seasons short during the decade. Teams couldn't afford to play the usual sixty-game season, so schedules were modified. It's worth noting that Parallel fielded an all-female team for two weeks during 1937. The male players were ill from food poisoning and the women of Parallel stepped up and played while the men recovered. The women swept Red Cloud during their brief time in the "show" and helped the Lions win their second consecutive pennant.

Certainly, the most bizarre season in K.R.A.P. history was 1939. League Commissioner Cornelius McGillicuddy tinkered with the rules in order to draw attention to the league. His mission was to take the league from independent status to a Class C affiliation with Major League Baseball.

His innovation was to modify the direction that runners took on the base paths. If a batter put the ball in play, he would run to third. If a batter walked or was hit by a pitch, he would go to first. Of course, this had disastrous effects when two runners were on at the same time because they would be running in opposite directions. Collisions near second base were common in 1939. Local newspapers began to include runner collisions in their box scores. The new rule also made it nearly impossible to turn a double play.

The rules only lasted one season. McGillicuddy was demoted, ironically, to Rules Enforcement and the league (although it got plenty of attention) failed to become affiliated with Major League Baseball. Vesper and Minden had the fewest players on the disabled list that season and thus finished first and second, respectively, in the league standings. With order restored, the K.R.A.P. League looked forward to the 1940s.

1940 – 1950

The Forties saw a resurgence of Gnomes. Geneva won back-to-back titles in '40 and '41. Red Cloud continued its success, winning three more pennants. However, the story of the decade was the Portis Eskimos. After nineteen years of futility, the Eskimos won the pennant in 1948. Proving they were not just a fluke, they won titles in '49 and 1950. After the 1950 season, the K.R.A.P. League folded. For more on the history of the league, visit **Kansaska.com**.

Appendix IV

The Real Portis, Kansas

By Marjorie Kirkpatrick

My Daddy always let people know just how special Portis is by explaining that it is the "middle of the middles". Portis is located seventeen miles north of the Geodetic Center of North America and 19 miles south of the Geographic Center of the forty eight states. It also has the longest main street in the world, since its main street is Highway 281, which stretches from Canada to Mexico. It has a famous cartoonist, Melvin "Tubby" Millar, who began his budding career way back in the Portis Schools in the early 1900s. He finally made his way to California and was hired by Warner Brothers, where he drew for Looney Tunes and made Porky Pig famous. But Porky Pig was around in Portis before he made it out to California.

In the 1940s, Portis had about three hundred residents. Its two-block-long main street had quite a variety of businesses available. The school was the social place to be for the entire community. Whether one had children in the school or not, everyone attended the games, operettas, programs and PTA. The PTA meetings were just another town social event for all to enjoy. One could visit with the teachers at such an event and the whole community knew if a child was having problems in school of any kind, so there were no parent-teacher conferences.

There were three churches in town, and since all were on Main Street, they were known as the North Church, the South Church, and the Methodist Church, which was located in between the North and South Churches. Rarely, were they referred to as the Church of the Brethren, the Methodist, and the First Brethren Church.

The highest hill north of town is known as Windy Point. Every Easter all three churches grouped together for a 5:00 a.m. Sunrise Service at the top of Windy Point. The low point, if there was such a thing, was east of town along a dry creek bed. This is known as Whiskey Hollow, which supposedly got its name supposedly from several men of the town sneaking down to the bridge there and drinking whiskey.

At the north edge of town where the highway curves west, there was the Honky Tonk Café. It burned down in the early '40s, and all that remained for many years was a pile of stone rubble. Gypsy bands would arrive in town each summer and camp at the Honky Tonk ruins. They would then converge on Portis businesses and take whatever they could sneak into their voluminous clothing. Many times they would knock on the doors of residents and keep them talking while two would sneak around back and steal from the garages or backs of the houses. Our mother would send my sister and me to the back porch, which was in full view of the driveway and garage, and tell us to watch out for anyone coming to the back of the house while she was trying to get rid of the people in front. No one had locks on their doors at that time.

Other interesting visitors to our safe little town were the hobos who alighted from the boxcars of the trains that stopped at the edge of town, near where we lived. They would knock on our back door and ask if they could work for food. Daddy told Mother to just send them to the Post Office (he was the Postmaster), and he would buy them a loaf of bread and some meat. The hobos only knocked on certain doors in town and always the same ones. We finally figured out that they would mark a tree in the yard of a home where people were kind to them, so the next ones would know where to stop.

Interesting characters that lived in Portis during the '40s: Slick Fleener, Fuzz Greaves, Rawls Garver, Curly Graham, Gubby Kaup, Shorty Wolters. We never thought their names were funny, because that is all we ever heard them called.

Portis grew in size every July when wheat harvest took place. One could see trucks lined up on Main Street from both directions waiting to have their loads of wheat weighed and dumped at the elevator. For two weeks each summer our town was abuzz with truckloads of beautiful golden wheat, combines moving through to get to another field and farmers' wives driving out to the fields with hot meals for their husbands who worked all day and into the night to complete the harvests.

Another time each summer when the town's population grew considerably was a two-week period when the annual tent revival meetings were held. Seven churches in the area met together and formed a revival committee. A huge tent was set up on a vacant lot behind the bank with a sawdust floor and huge stage. A well-known guest evangelist and music leader would be invited to come and hold revival meetings every evening during that two-week period. During the day, the seven churches sent teachers to the public school to hold vacation Bible school. Rawls Garver would sleep under the stage on the sawdust every night to guard the piano, microphones and music equipment.

The Missouri Pacific Railroad ran through the north end of town. Long lines of boxcars trailed behind the engines waiting to be filled with wheat from the elevator. Everyday the passenger/mail train known as the Doodlebug passed through and stopped at the depot to deposit mail bags onto a huge open hay wagon, which Rawls Garver then would pull downhill to the Post Office. In the early spring there often were large boxes of fluffy yellow baby chicks poking their beaks out of little breathing holes and cheeping continually. Farmers would order the chicks by mail and each box might contain as many as a hundred of them.

Our schoolhouse on the east side of town had no gym or place to hold town meetings, so an old barn/stable just west of Main Street was converted into a gym/meeting room. All of our basketball games were held in this old barn with a wooden floor. Each school year, the students put on an operetta for the town in the same drafty tin barn, and on the last day of school, the entire town turned out for a potluck dinner there. The homemade food brought out all the residents in the area whether they had school-age children or not. When the barn wasn't being used for games or meetings, we were allowed to roller skate in there.

The hospital was located east of the school grounds. It was a magnificent huge building designed and built by Doctor Claude Burtch. He had a wooden leg that he had made himself and it creaked when he walked. He was well known in an area of counties quite a distance away, and people from all over the area came to the hospital for treatment. The main floor of the hospital was his family's living quarters with beautiful hardwood floors, a grand piano, and a huge open staircase that led to the second floor where patient's rooms and the surgery were located.

Doc Burtch was rather a tough old bird and uncouth in his language, but he knew his medicine. He trained his nurses himself. When television came on the scene in the early 1950s, he was the first one to have a television set in Portis. He installed the high antenna tower atop the hospital himself, climbing the roof and the tower in spite of his wooden leg. My sister and I had the first dose of penicillin when it came out. It was in powder form and shot down the throat by squeezing a huge eyedropper gadget. It is amazing we didn't choke or suffocate with such a procedure!

On the west end of town and on a farm south of town, two men raised greyhounds, which were raced all over the country. When the moon was full, we would hear coyotes up on the hill behind our house baying at the moon, which would set off the greyhounds on the opposite end of town. It probably was the first "stereo system" known at that time.

Toys were pretty simple then. Since my sister and I grew up near the tracks, we collected a lot of loose railroad spikes and put them to use with a lot of imagination. There also were wooden crates in which oranges were shipped. Each one had a divider down the middle, but if turned up on end, they made great shelves, cupboards, storage units, etc. The trees surrounding our house became a jungle for swinging from branch to branch or for curling up and reading. Bicycles, roller-skates, and stilts were the mode of transportation for kids. My stilts were made from a set of bed slats. No one missed school unless they had scarlet fever, measles or mumps. It was just expected that one get a perfect attendance award at the end of the year. On snow days all the town kids walked to school anyway, and the farm kids rode ponies or tractors to school if the roads were too bad for being driven by car or pickup.

On Main Street one could find all the business owners' cars parked in front of their businesses with the keys in the ignition. If the old retired gents walked uptown for their mail, they would sit on an old wooden bench in front of Doc Burtch's office on Main Street or climb into one of the cars and sit awhile.

It sure doesn't look like this now, but I do hope it makes you want to visit sometime.

—Marjorie

Author's Note: Marge Kirkpatrick grew up in Portis and served as my technical advisor on this project. I took a few creative licenses with the description of the town, but Marge is pretty cool so I think she didn't mind. She lives in Omaha now, which makes her house the best bed and breakfast around during the College World Series. She and her husband Larry are two of the finest people you will ever meet. —J S

*This novel was set in Palatino
using Adobe InDesign CS3.*

*Friends don't let friends use
Papyrus or Microsoft Word.*